W9-BBA-623

DISCARD

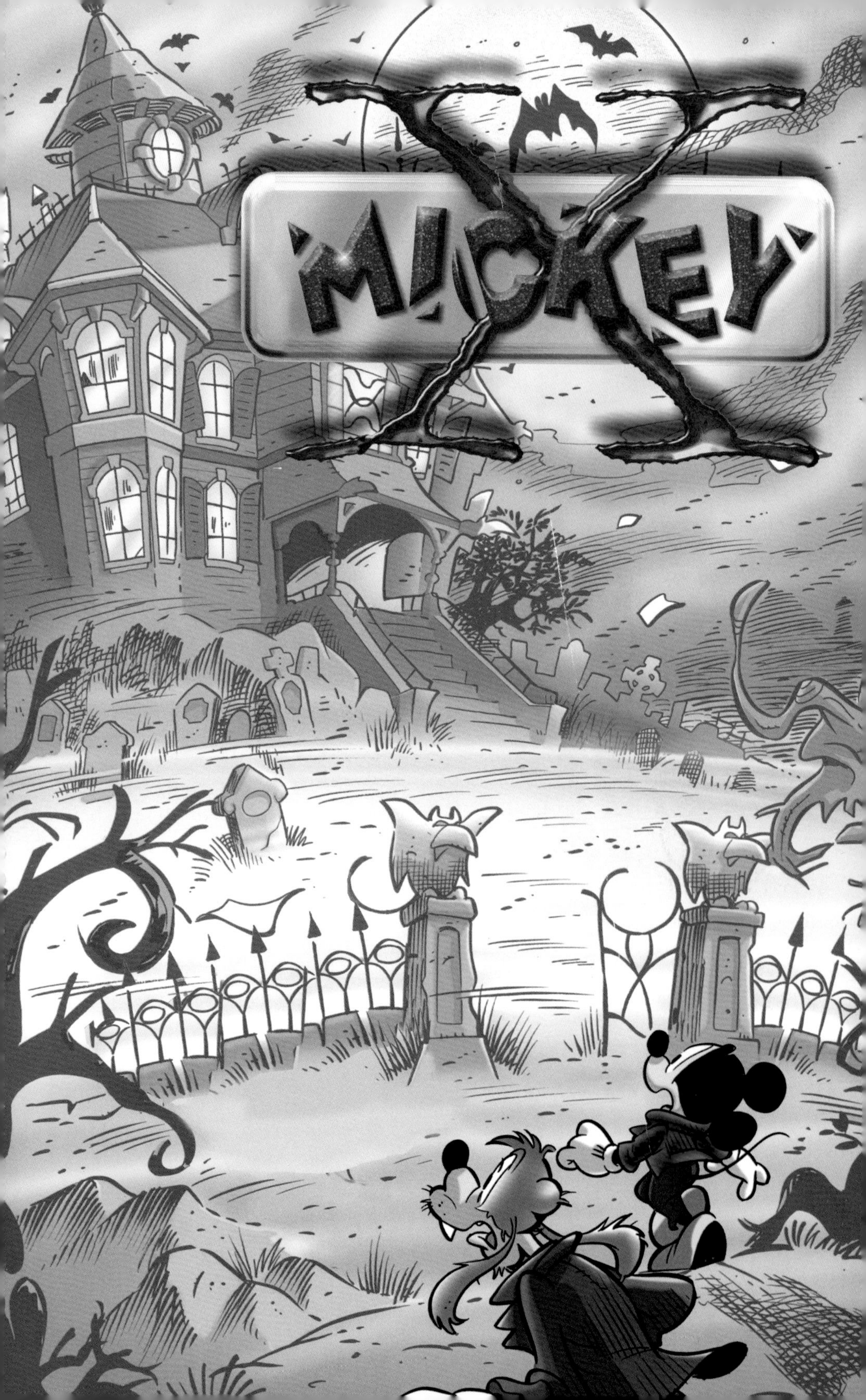
MICKEY
X

# Graphic Novels Available from
# PAPERCUTZ

**Graphic Novel #1**
"Prilla's Talent"

**Graphic Novel #2**
"Tinker Bell and the
Wings of Rani"

**Graphic Novel #3**
"Tinker Bell and the
Day of the Dragon"

**Graphic Novel #4**
"Tinker Bell
to the Rescue"

**Graphic Novel #5**
"Tinker Bell and the
Pirate Adventure"

**Graphic Novel #6**
"A Present
for Tinker Bell"

**Graphic Novel #7**
"Tinker Bell the
Perfect Fairy"

**Graphic Novel #8**
"Tinker Bell and her
Stories for a Rainy Day"

**Graphic Novel #9**
"Tinker Bell and
her Magical Arrival"

**Graphic Novel #10**
"Tinker Bell and
the Lucky Rainbow"

**Graphic Novel #11**
"Tinker Bell and the
Most Precious Gift"

**Graphic Novel #12**
"Tinker Bell and the
Lost Treasure"

**Graphic Novel #13**
"Tinker Bell and the
Pixie Hollow Games"

**Graphic Novel #14**
"Tinker Bell and
Blaze"

**Tinker Bell
and the Great
Fairy Rescue**

**Graphic Novel #15**
"Tinker Bell and the
Secret of the Wings"

**Graphic Novel #16**
"Tinker Bell and the
Pirate Fairy"

**Graphic Novel #17**
"Tinker Bell and the
Legend of the NeverBeast"

**Graphic Novel #18**
"Tinker Bell and her
Magical Friends"

DISNEY FAIRIES graphic novels are available in paperback for $7.99 each;
in hardcover for $12.99 each except #5, $6.99PB, $10.99HC. #6-14 are $7.99PB $11.99HC.
#15 – 18 are $7.99PB $12.99HC.
Tinker Bell and the Great Fairy Rescue is $9.99 in hardcover only.
Available at booksellers everywhere.

## See more at papercutz.com

Or you can order from us: Please add $4.00 for postage and handling for first book, and add $1.00 for each additional book.
Please make check payable to NBM Publishing. Send to: Papercutz, 160 Broadway, Suite 700, East Wing, New York, NY 10038
or call 800 886 1223 (9-6 EST M-F) MC-Visa-Amex accepted.

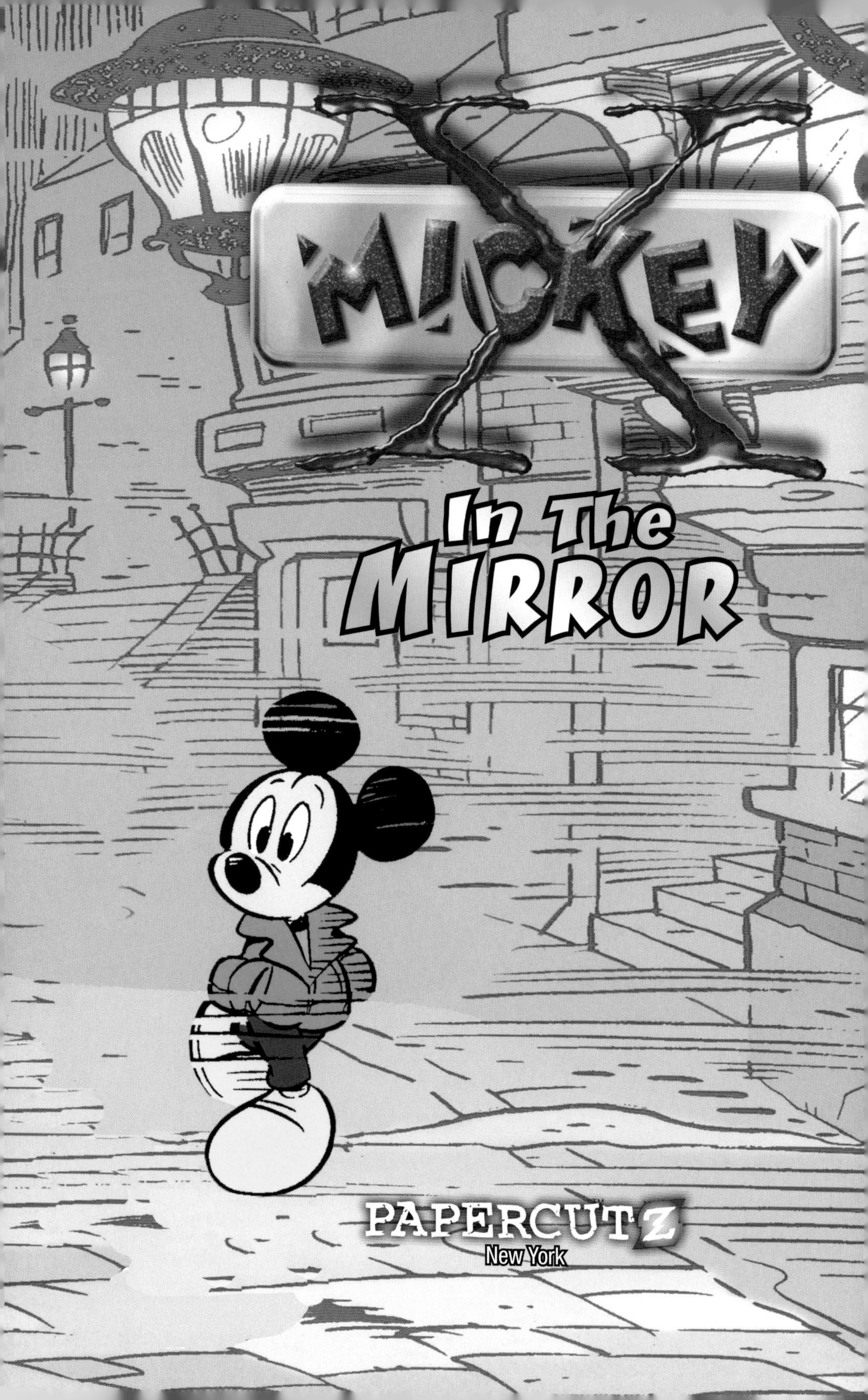
MICKEY X
In The MIRROR
PAPERCUTZ
New York

# CONTENTS

DISNEY GRAPHIC NOVELS #2 "X-Mickey"
"In the Mirror"

Bruno Enna – Writer
Alessandro Perina – Artist
Dawn Guzzo – Production
Jeff Whitman – Production Coordinator
Robert V. Conte – Editor
Bethany Bryan – Associate Editor
Jim Salicrup
Editor-in-Chief

ISBN: 978-162991-446-6 Paperback Edition
ISBN: 978-162991-447-3 Hardcover Edition

Copyright © 2016 by Disney Enterprises, Inc. All rights reserved.

Printed in Canada
March 2016 by Friesens Printing
1 Printers Way
Altona, MB ROG 0B0

Papercutz books may be purchased for business or promotional use.
For information on bulk purchases please contact Macmillan Corporate
and Premium Sales Department at
(800) 221-7945 x 5442.

Distributed by Macmillan
Second Papercutz Printing

FSC
www.fsc.org
MIX
Paper from
responsible sources
FSC® C016245

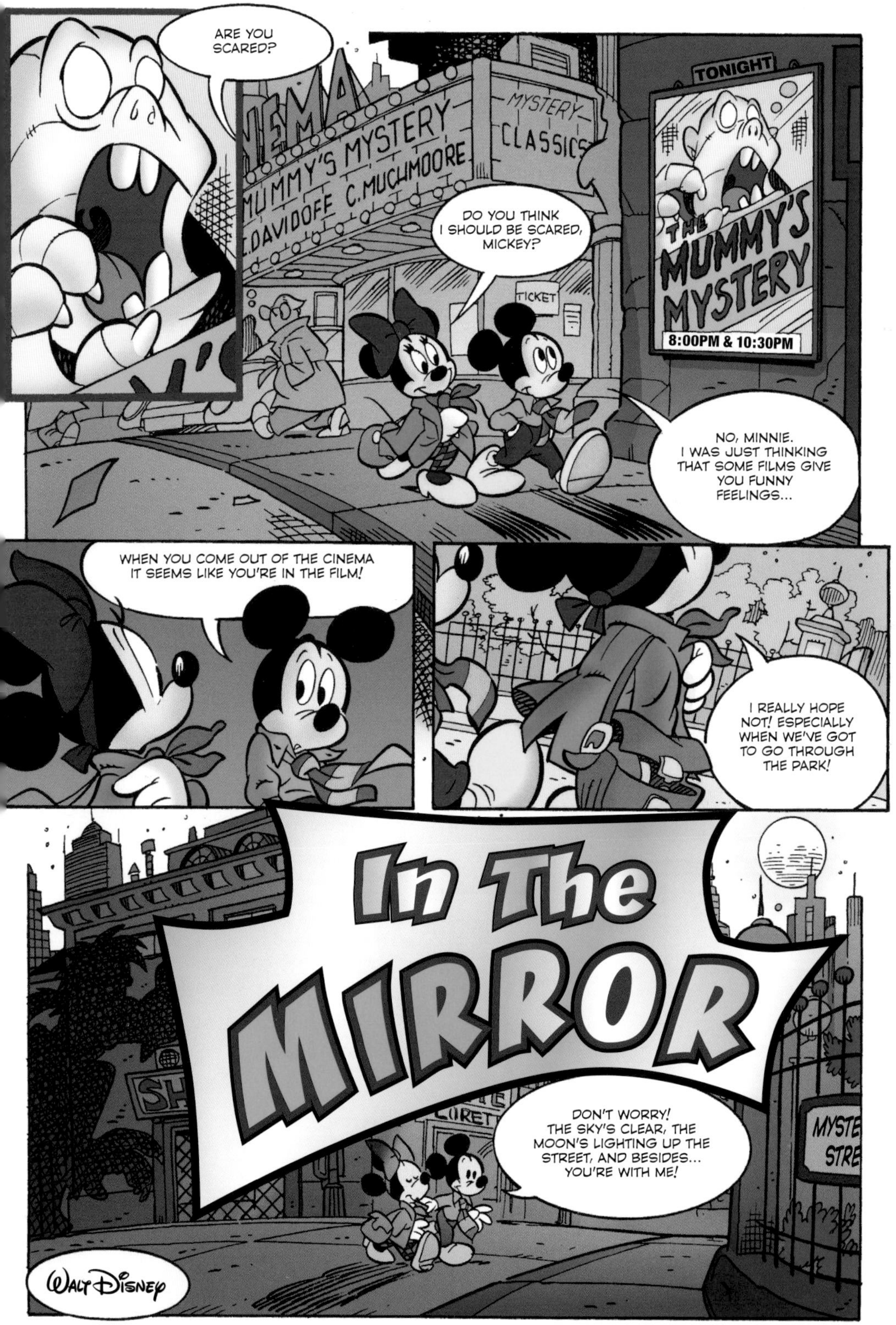
ARE YOU SCARED?
MUMMY'S MYSTERY
C.DAVIDOFF C.MUCHMOORE
MYSTERY CLASSICS
TONIGHT
THE MUMMY'S MYSTERY
8:00PM & 10:30PM
TICKET
DO YOU THINK I SHOULD BE SCARED, MICKEY?
NO, MINNIE. I WAS JUST THINKING THAT SOME FILMS GIVE YOU FUNNY FEELINGS...
WHEN YOU COME OUT OF THE CINEMA IT SEEMS LIKE YOU'RE IN THE FILM!
I REALLY HOPE NOT! ESPECIALLY WHEN WE'VE GOT TO GO THROUGH THE PARK!
In The MIRROR
DON'T WORRY! THE SKY'S CLEAR, THE MOON'S LIGHTING UP THE STREET, AND BESIDES... YOU'RE WITH ME!
WALT DISNEY

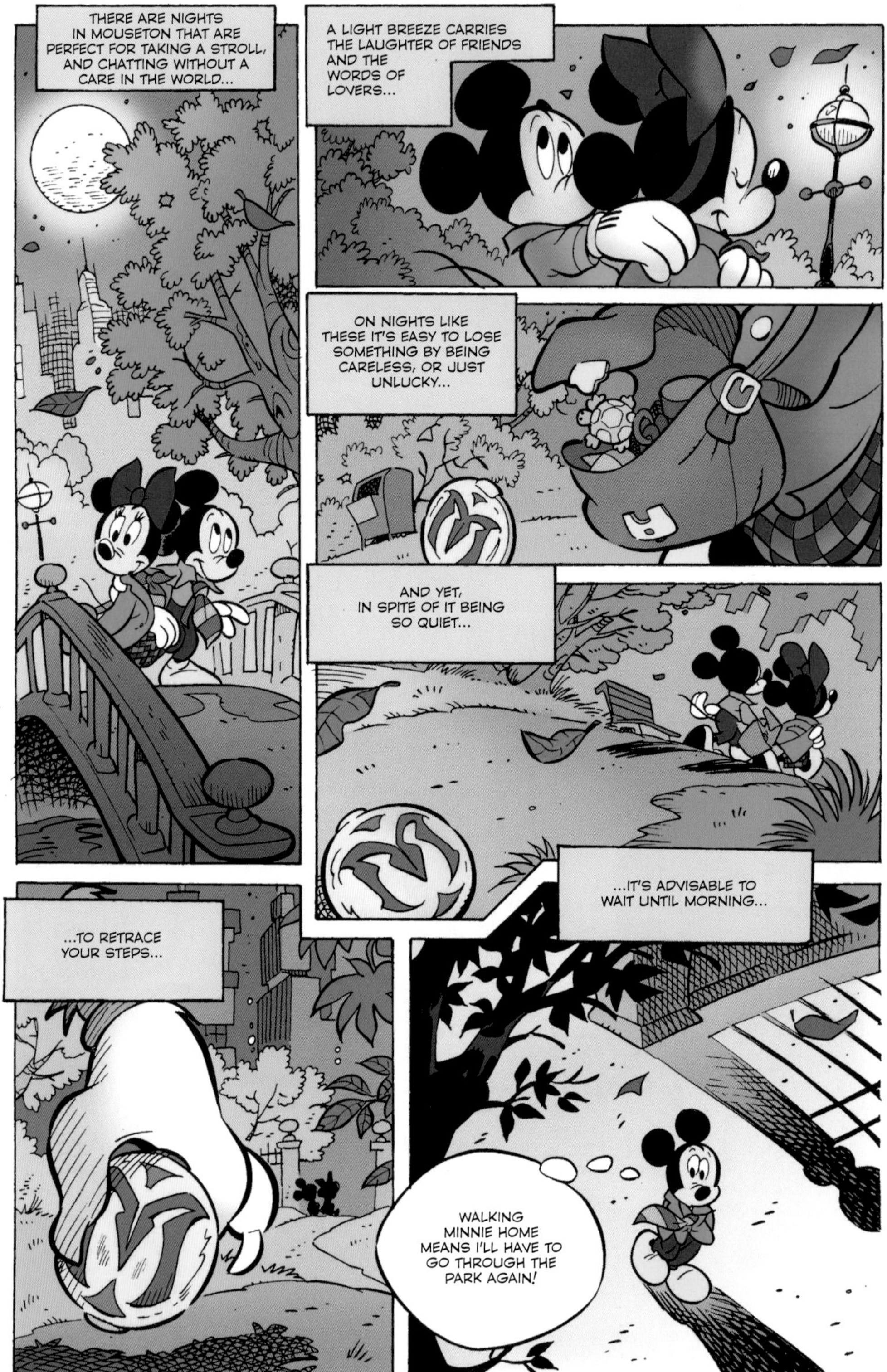
THERE ARE NIGHTS IN MOUSETON THAT ARE PERFECT FOR TAKING A STROLL, AND CHATTING WITHOUT A CARE IN THE WORLD...
A LIGHT BREEZE CARRIES THE LAUGHTER OF FRIENDS AND THE WORDS OF LOVERS...
ON NIGHTS LIKE THESE IT'S EASY TO LOSE SOMETHING BY BEING CARELESS, OR JUST UNLUCKY...
AND YET, IN SPITE OF IT BEING SO QUIET...
...TO RETRACE YOUR STEPS...
...IT'S ADVISABLE TO WAIT UNTIL MORNING...
WALKING MINNIE HOME MEANS I'LL HAVE TO GO THROUGH THE PARK AGAIN!

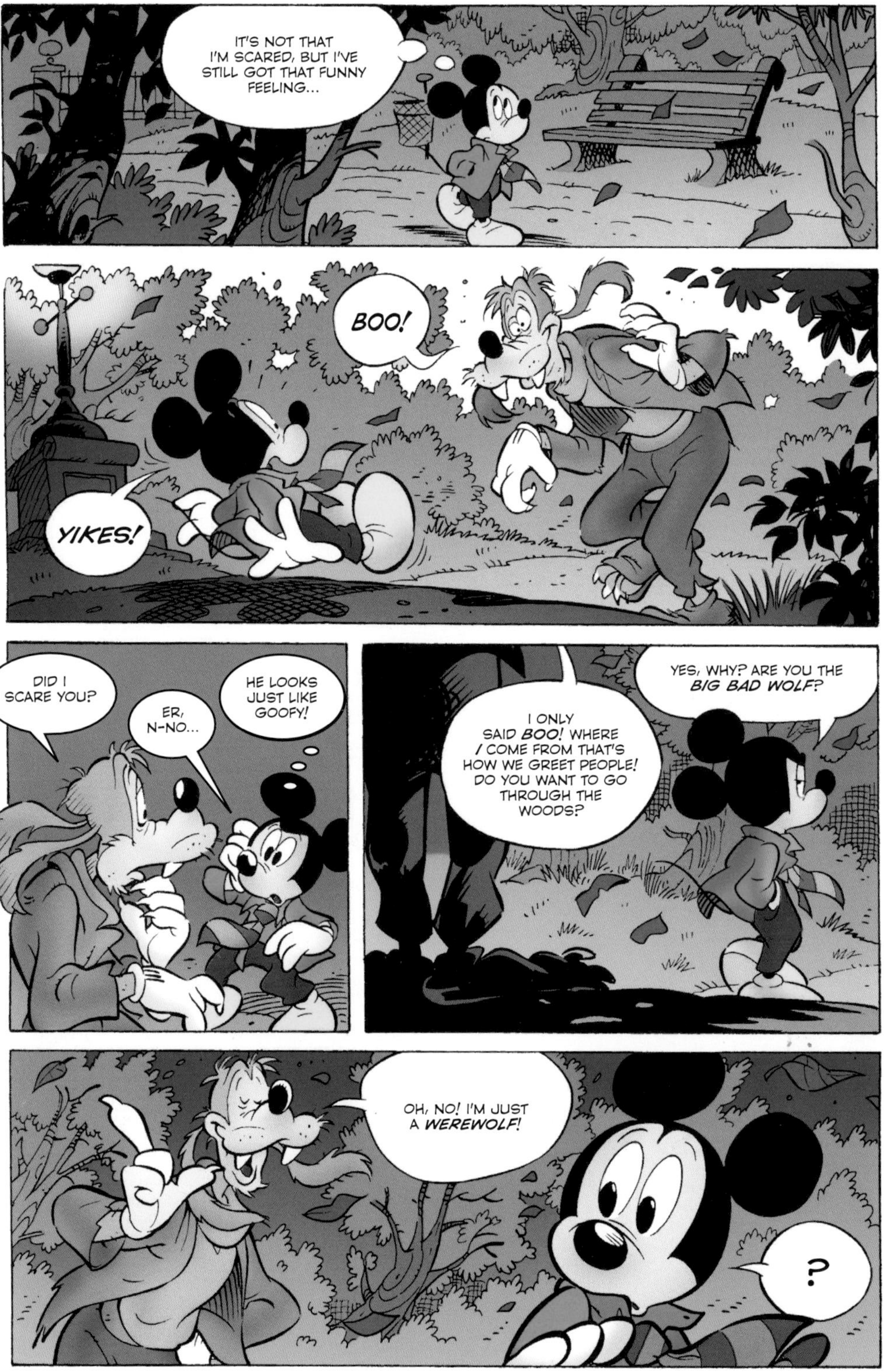

IT'S NOT THAT I'M SCARED, BUT I'VE STILL GOT THAT FUNNY FEELING...
BOO!
YIKES!
DID I SCARE YOU?
ER, N-NO...
HE LOOKS JUST LIKE GOOFY!
YES, WHY? ARE YOU THE *BIG BAD WOLF*?
I ONLY SAID *BOO!* WHERE *I* COME FROM THAT'S HOW WE GREET PEOPLE! DO YOU WANT TO GO THROUGH THE WOODS?
OH, NO! I'M JUST A *WEREWOLF*!
?

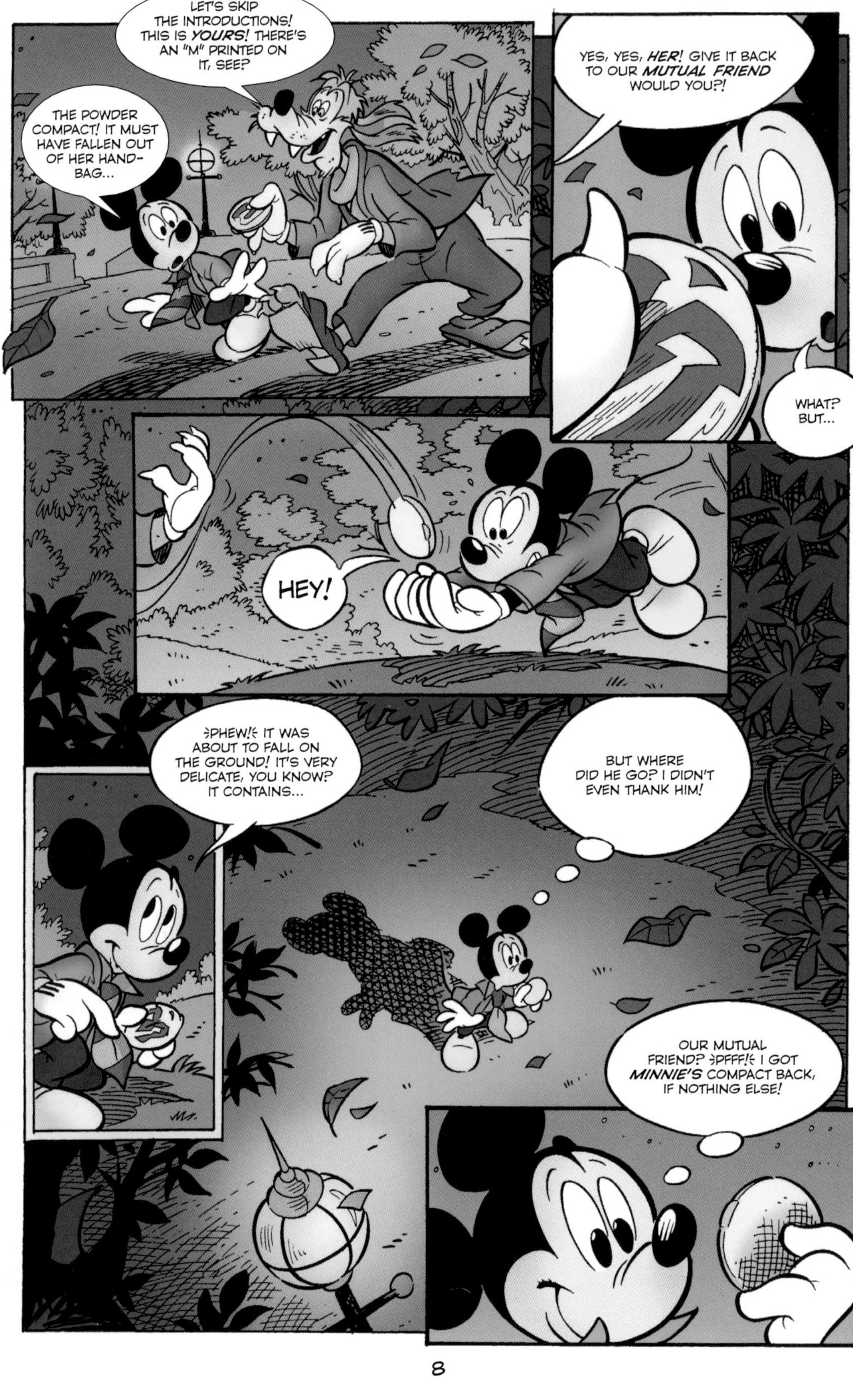
THE POWDER COMPACT! IT MUST HAVE FALLEN OUT OF HER HAND-BAG...
LET'S SKIP THE INTRODUCTIONS! THIS IS YOURS! THERE'S AN "M" PRINTED ON IT, SEE?
YES, YES, HER! GIVE IT BACK TO OUR MUTUAL FRIEND WOULD YOU?!
WHAT? BUT...
HEY!
PHEW! IT WAS ABOUT TO FALL ON THE GROUND! IT'S VERY DELICATE, YOU KNOW? IT CONTAINS...
BUT WHERE DID HE GO? I DIDN'T EVEN THANK HIM!
OUR MUTUAL FRIEND? PFFF! I GOT MINNIE'S COMPACT BACK, IF NOTHING ELSE!

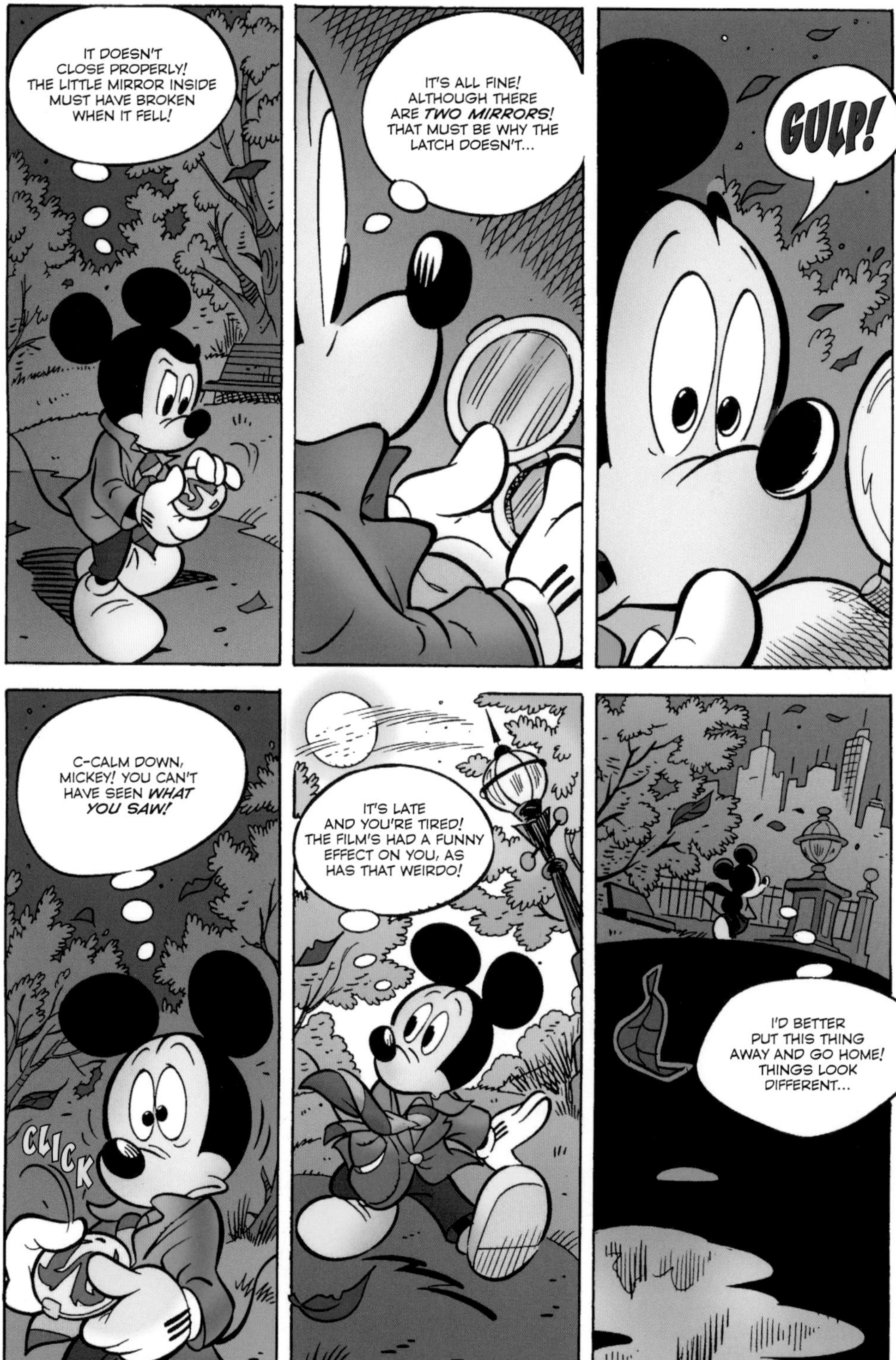
IT DOESN'T CLOSE PROPERLY! THE LITTLE MIRROR INSIDE MUST HAVE BROKEN WHEN IT FELL!
IT'S ALL FINE! ALTHOUGH THERE ARE *TWO MIRRORS!* THAT MUST BE WHY THE LATCH DOESN'T...
GULP!
C-CALM DOWN, MICKEY! YOU CAN'T HAVE SEEN *WHAT YOU SAW!*
CLICK
IT'S LATE AND YOU'RE TIRED! THE FILM'S HAD A FUNNY EFFECT ON YOU, AS HAS THAT WEIRDO!
I'D BETTER PUT THIS THING AWAY AND GO HOME! THINGS LOOK DIFFERENT...

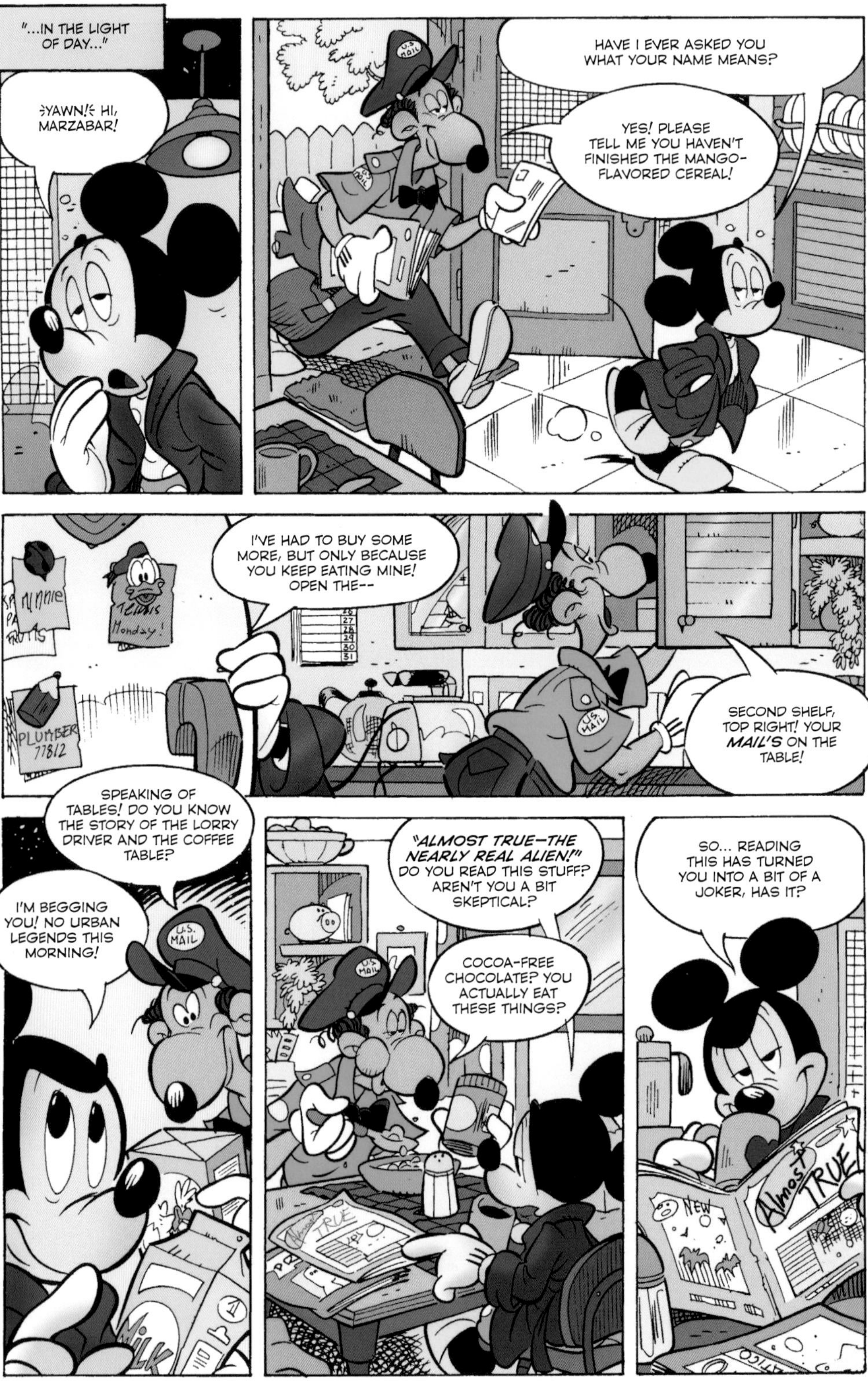

"...IN THE LIGHT OF DAY..."
YAWN! HI, MARZABAR!
HAVE I EVER ASKED YOU WHAT YOUR NAME MEANS?
YES! PLEASE TELL ME YOU HAVEN'T FINISHED THE MANGO-FLAVORED CEREAL!
I'VE HAD TO BUY SOME MORE, BUT ONLY BECAUSE YOU KEEP EATING MINE! OPEN THE--
SECOND SHELF, TOP RIGHT! YOUR ***MAIL'S*** ON THE TABLE!
SPEAKING OF TABLES! DO YOU KNOW THE STORY OF THE LORRY DRIVER AND THE COFFEE TABLE?
I'M BEGGING YOU! NO URBAN LEGENDS THIS MORNING!
***"ALMOST TRUE—THE NEARLY REAL ALIEN!"*** DO YOU READ THIS STUFF? AREN'T YOU A BIT SKEPTICAL?
COCOA-FREE CHOCOLATE? YOU ACTUALLY EAT THESE THINGS?
SO... READING THIS HAS TURNED YOU INTO A BIT OF A JOKER, HAS IT?

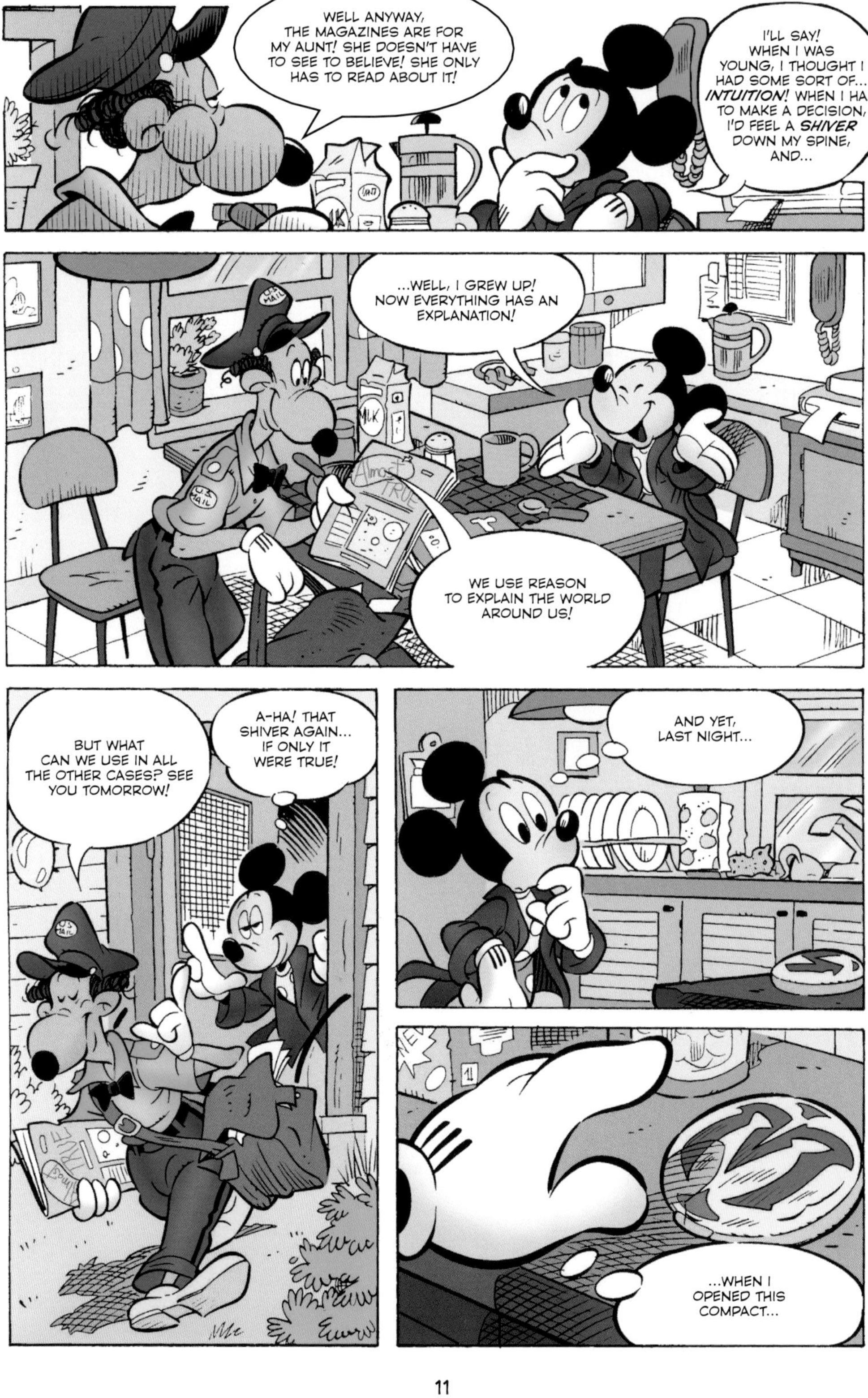
WELL ANYWAY, THE MAGAZINES ARE FOR MY AUNT! SHE DOESN'T HAVE TO SEE TO BELIEVE! SHE ONLY HAS TO READ ABOUT IT!
I'LL SAY! WHEN I WAS YOUNG, I THOUGHT I HAD SOME SORT OF... *INTUITION!* WHEN I HAD TO MAKE A DECISION, I'D FEEL A *SHIVER* DOWN MY SPINE, AND...
...WELL, I GREW UP! NOW EVERYTHING HAS AN EXPLANATION!
WE USE REASON TO EXPLAIN THE WORLD AROUND US!
BUT WHAT CAN WE USE IN ALL THE OTHER CASES? SEE YOU TOMORROW!
A-HA! THAT SHIVER AGAIN... IF ONLY IT WERE TRUE!
AND YET, LAST NIGHT...
...WHEN I OPENED THIS COMPACT...

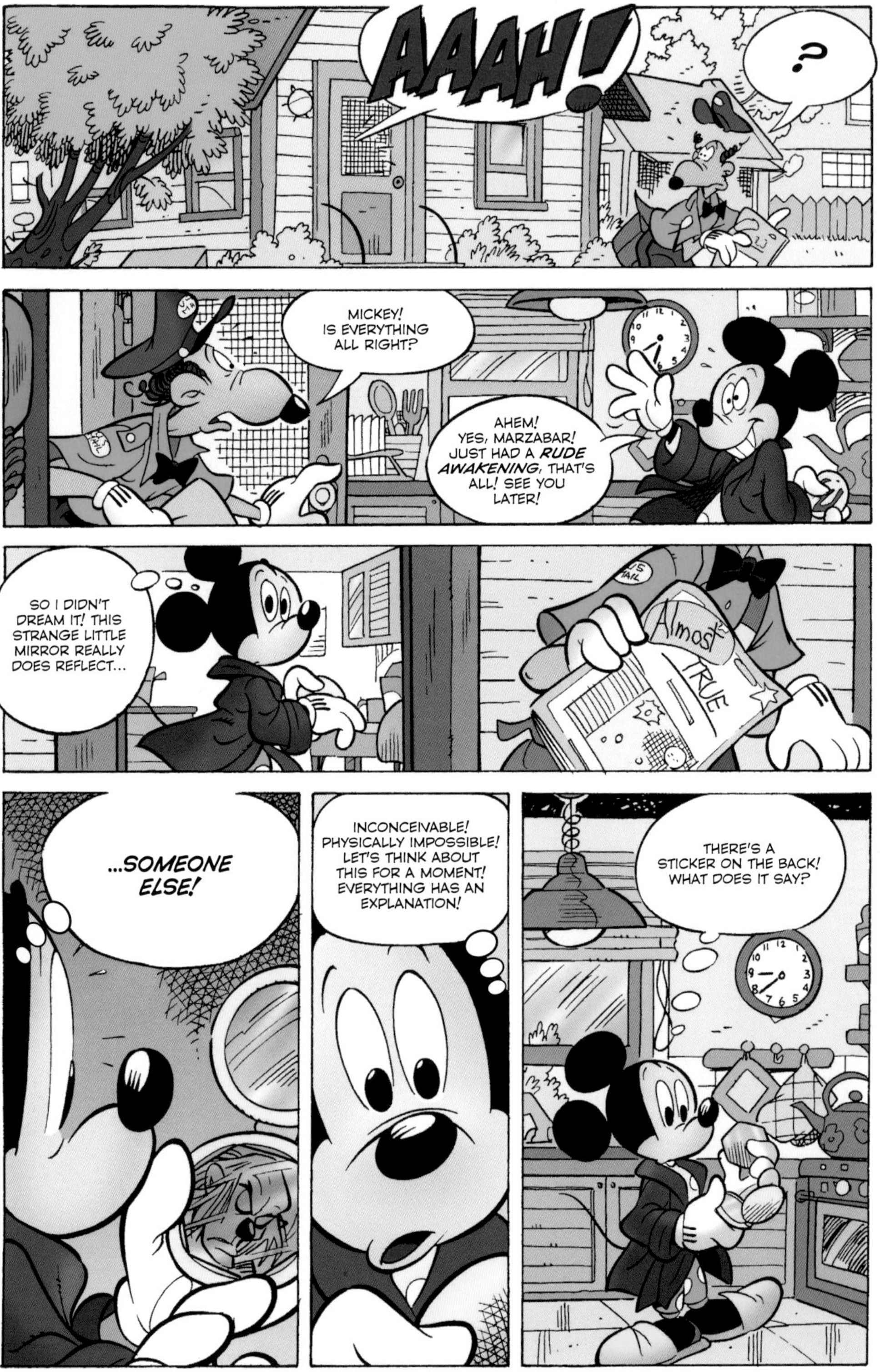
AAAH!
?
MICKEY! IS EVERYTHING ALL RIGHT?
AHEM! YES, MARZABAR! JUST HAD A **RUDE AWAKENING**, THAT'S ALL! SEE YOU LATER!
SO I DIDN'T DREAM IT! THIS STRANGE LITTLE MIRROR REALLY DOES REFLECT...
Almost TRUE
...SOMEONE ELSE!
INCONCEIVABLE! PHYSICALLY IMPOSSIBLE! LET'S THINK ABOUT THIS FOR A MOMENT! EVERYTHING HAS AN EXPLANATION!
THERE'S A STICKER ON THE BACK! WHAT DOES IT SAY?

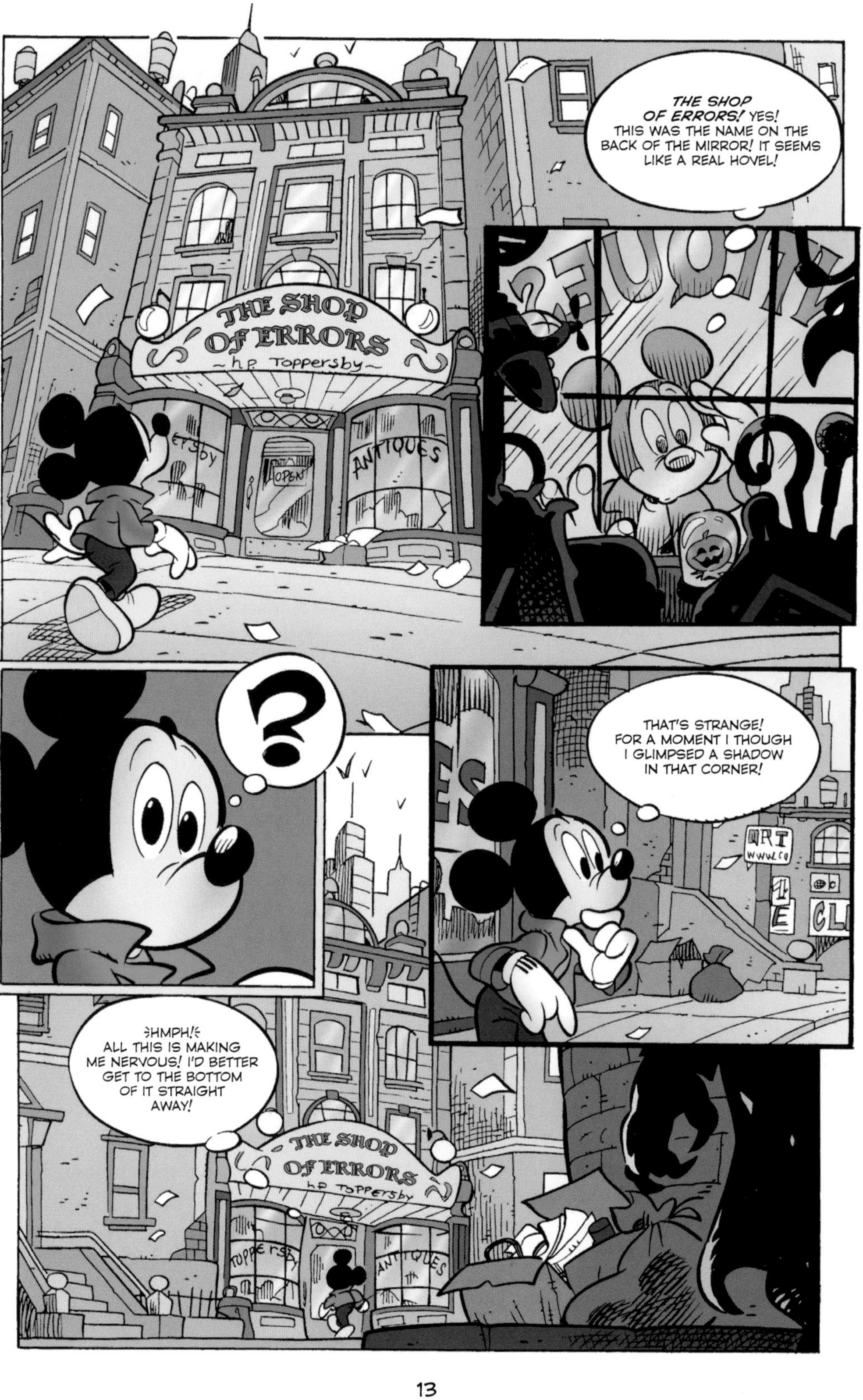
THE SHOP OF ERRORS! YES! THIS WAS THE NAME ON THE BACK OF THE MIRROR! IT SEEMS LIKE A REAL HOVEL!
THE SHOP OF ERRORS
~h.p. Toppersby~
ANTIQUES
OPEN
?
THAT'S STRANGE! FOR A MOMENT I THOUGH I GLIMPSED A SHADOW IN THAT CORNER!
HMPH! ALL THIS IS MAKING ME NERVOUS! I'D BETTER GET TO THE BOTTOM OF IT STRAIGHT AWAY!
THE SHOP OF ERRORS
h.p. Toppersby
ANTIQUES

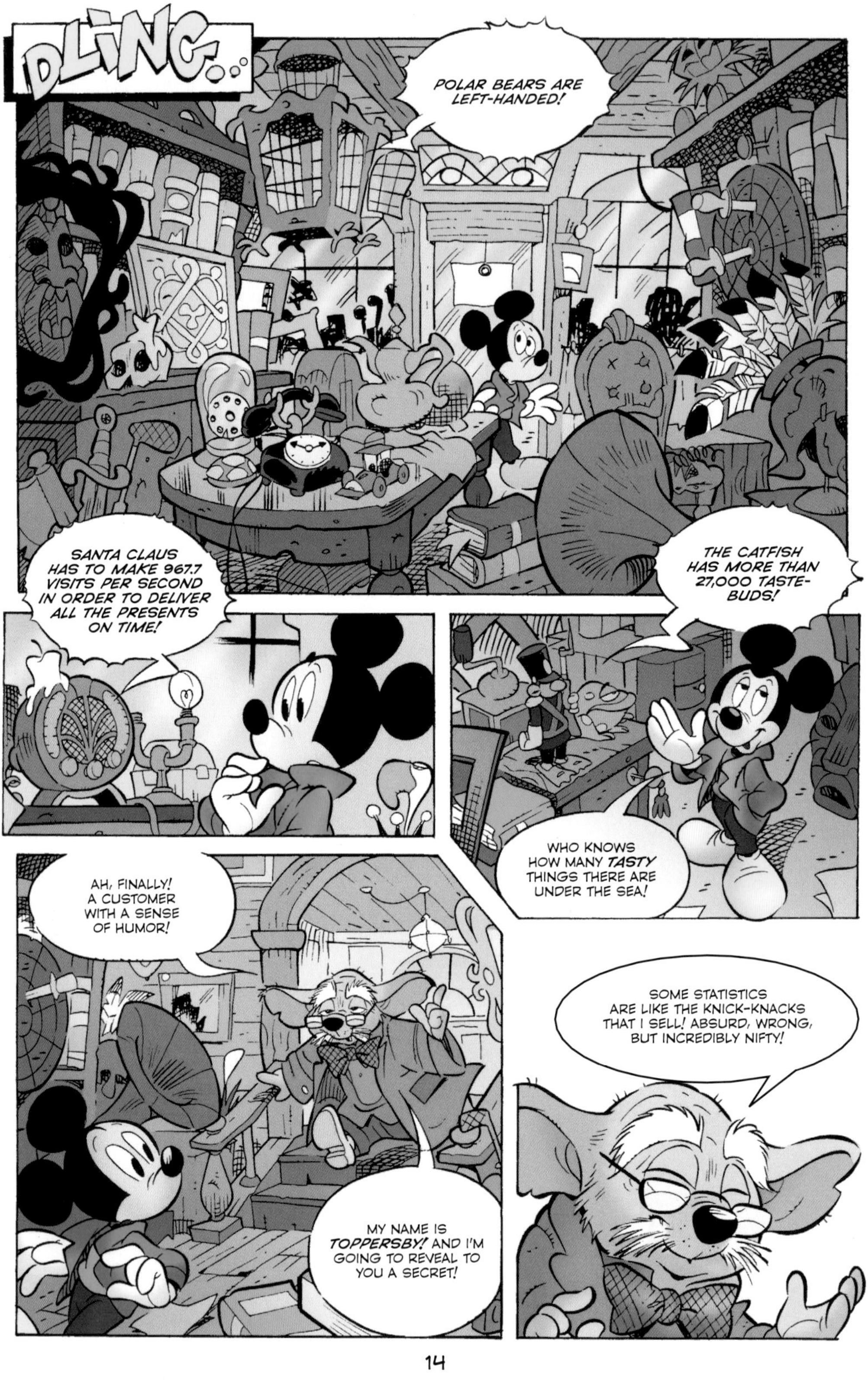
DLING...
POLAR BEARS ARE LEFT-HANDED!
SANTA CLAUS HAS TO MAKE 967.7 VISITS PER SECOND IN ORDER TO DELIVER ALL THE PRESENTS ON TIME!
THE CATFISH HAS MORE THAN 27,000 TASTE-BUDS!
WHO KNOWS HOW MANY *TASTY* THINGS THERE ARE UNDER THE SEA!
AH, FINALLY! A CUSTOMER WITH A SENSE OF HUMOR!
MY NAME IS *TOPPERSBY!* AND I'M GOING TO REVEAL TO YOU A SECRET!
SOME STATISTICS ARE LIKE THE KNICK-KNACKS THAT I SELL! ABSURD, WRONG, BUT INCREDIBLY NIFTY!

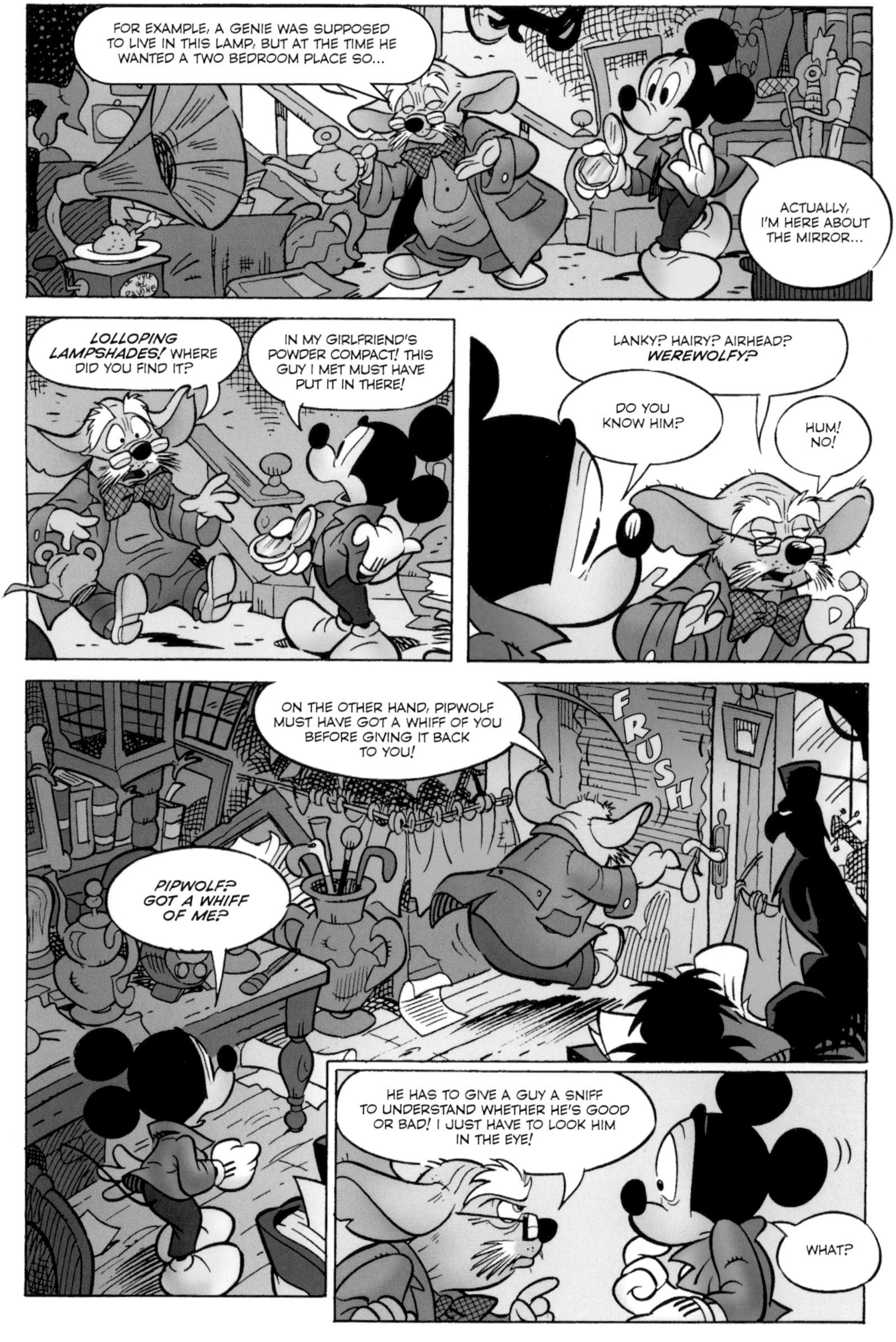
FOR EXAMPLE, A GENIE WAS SUPPOSED TO LIVE IN THIS LAMP, BUT AT THE TIME HE WANTED A TWO BEDROOM PLACE SO...
ACTUALLY, I'M HERE ABOUT THE MIRROR...
LOLLOPING LAMPSHADES! WHERE DID YOU FIND IT?
IN MY GIRLFRIEND'S POWDER COMPACT! THIS GUY I MET MUST HAVE PUT IT IN THERE!
LANKY? HAIRY? AIRHEAD? WEREWOLFY?
DO YOU KNOW HIM?
HUM! NO!
ON THE OTHER HAND, PIPWOLF MUST HAVE GOT A WHIFF OF YOU BEFORE GIVING IT BACK TO YOU!
FRUSH
PIPWOLF? GOT A WHIFF OF ME?
HE HAS TO GIVE A GUY A SNIFF TO UNDERSTAND WHETHER HE'S GOOD OR BAD! I JUST HAVE TO LOOK HIM IN THE EYE!
WHAT?

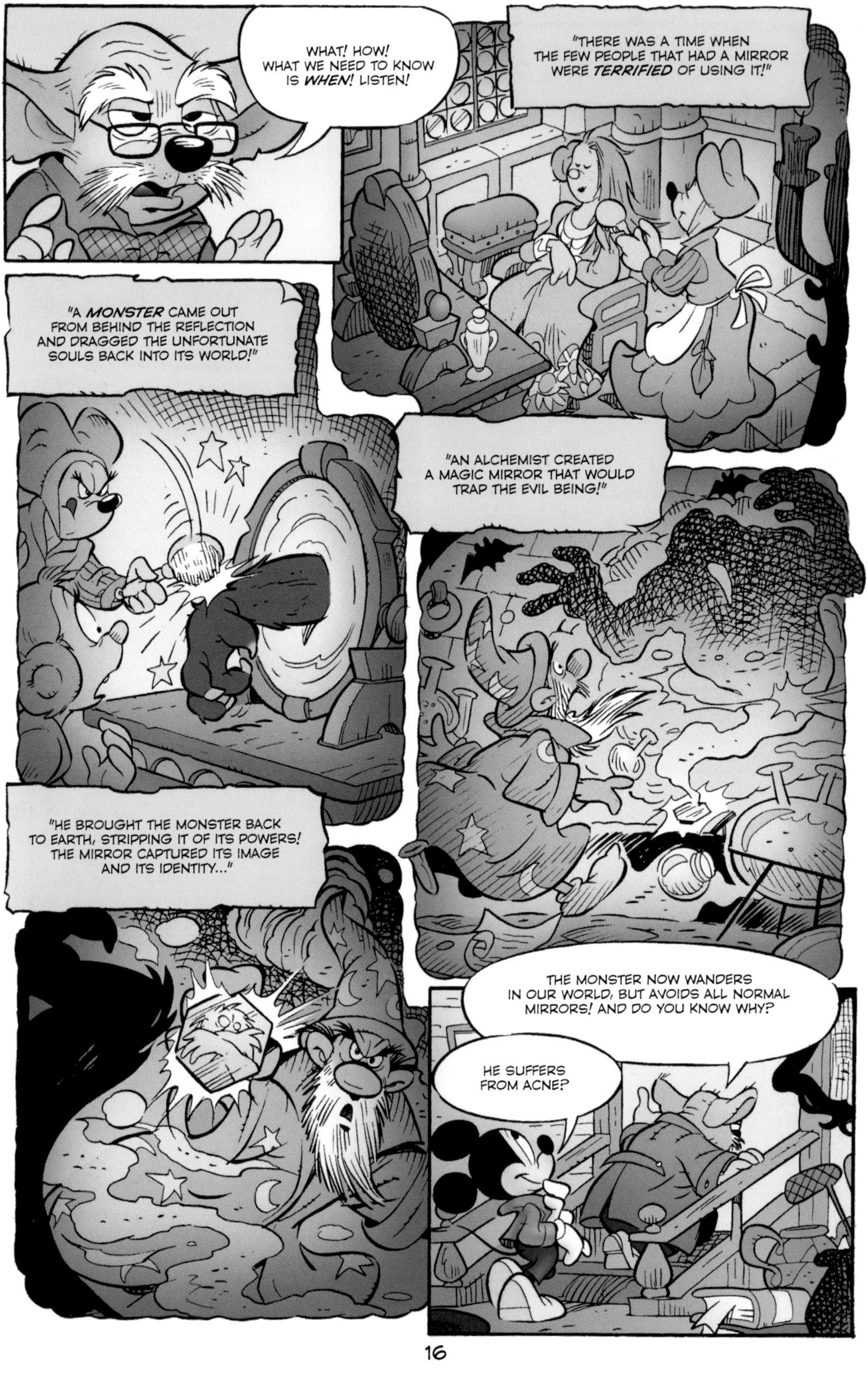
WHAT! HOW!
WHAT WE NEED TO KNOW
IS *WHEN*! LISTEN!
"THERE WAS A TIME WHEN
THE FEW PEOPLE THAT HAD A MIRROR
WERE *TERRIFIED* OF USING IT!"
"A *MONSTER* CAME OUT
FROM BEHIND THE REFLECTION
AND DRAGGED THE UNFORTUNATE
SOULS BACK INTO ITS WORLD!"
"AN ALCHEMIST CREATED
A MAGIC MIRROR THAT WOULD
TRAP THE EVIL BEING!"
"HE BROUGHT THE MONSTER BACK
TO EARTH, STRIPPING IT OF ITS POWERS!
THE MIRROR CAPTURED ITS IMAGE
AND ITS IDENTITY..."
THE MONSTER NOW WANDERS
IN OUR WORLD, BUT AVOIDS ALL NORMAL
MIRRORS! AND DO YOU KNOW WHY?
HE SUFFERS
FROM ACNE?

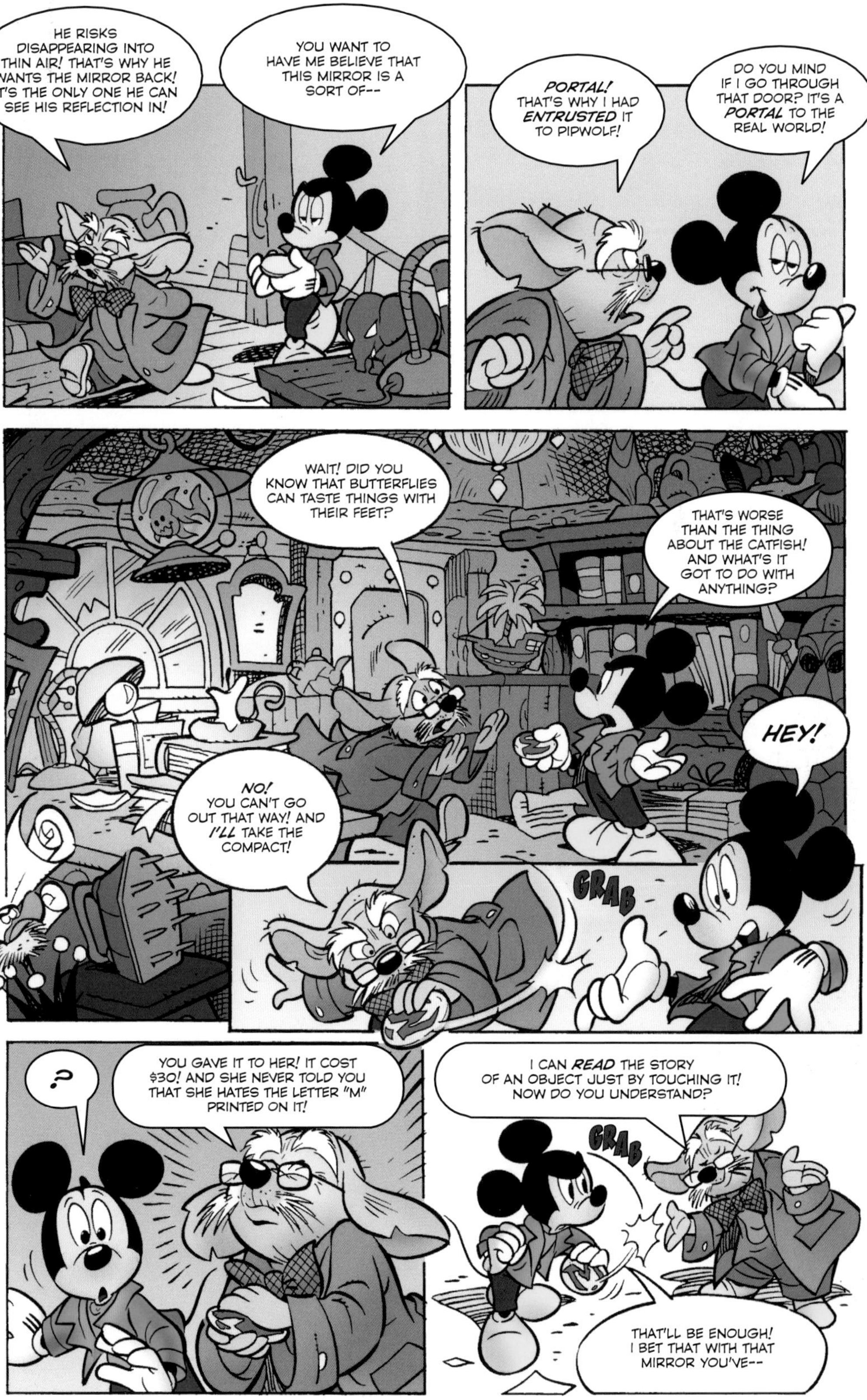
HE RISKS DISAPPEARING INTO THIN AIR! THAT'S WHY HE WANTS THE MIRROR BACK! IT'S THE ONLY ONE HE CAN SEE HIS REFLECTION IN!
YOU WANT TO HAVE ME BELIEVE THAT THIS MIRROR IS A SORT OF--
PORTAL! THAT'S WHY I HAD ENTRUSTED IT TO PIPWOLF!
DO YOU MIND IF I GO THROUGH THAT DOOR? IT'S A PORTAL TO THE REAL WORLD!
WAIT! DID YOU KNOW THAT BUTTERFLIES CAN TASTE THINGS WITH THEIR FEET?
THAT'S WORSE THAN THE THING ABOUT THE CATFISH! AND WHAT'S IT GOT TO DO WITH ANYTHING?
HEY!
NO! YOU CAN'T GO OUT THAT WAY! AND I'LL TAKE THE COMPACT!
GRAB
?
YOU GAVE IT TO HER! IT COST $30! AND SHE NEVER TOLD YOU THAT SHE HATES THE LETTER "M" PRINTED ON IT!
I CAN READ THE STORY OF AN OBJECT JUST BY TOUCHING IT! NOW DO YOU UNDERSTAND?
GRAB
THAT'LL BE ENOUGH! I BET THAT WITH THAT MIRROR YOU'VE--

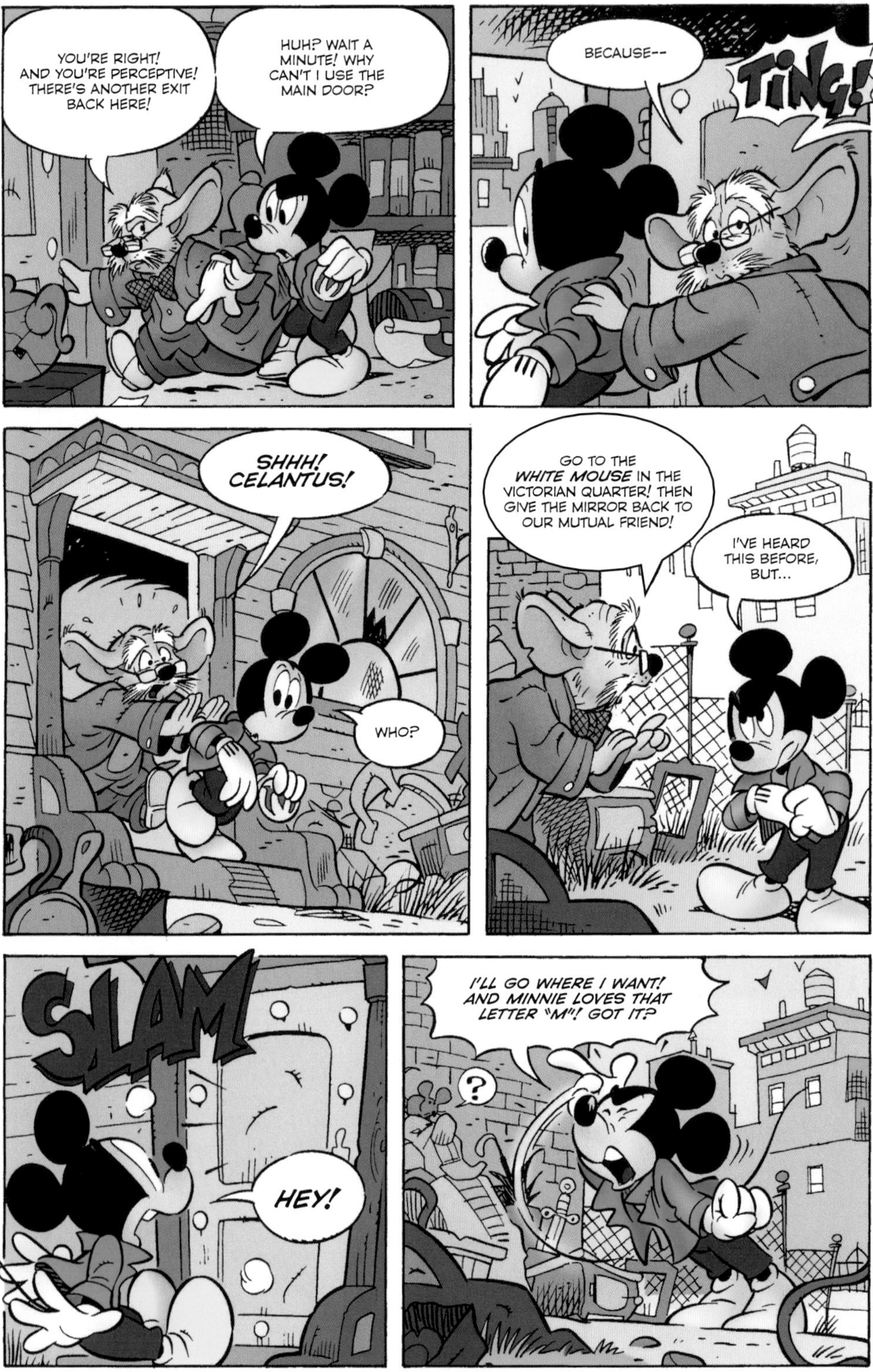
YOU'RE RIGHT! AND YOU'RE PERCEPTIVE! THERE'S ANOTHER EXIT BACK HERE!
HUH? WAIT A MINUTE! WHY CAN'T I USE THE MAIN DOOR?
BECAUSE--
TING!
SHHH! CELANTUS!
WHO?
GO TO THE WHITE MOUSE IN THE VICTORIAN QUARTER! THEN GIVE THE MIRROR BACK TO OUR MUTUAL FRIEND!
I'VE HEARD THIS BEFORE, BUT...
SLAM
HEY!
I'LL GO WHERE I WANT! AND MINNIE LOVES THAT LETTER "M"! GOT IT?
?

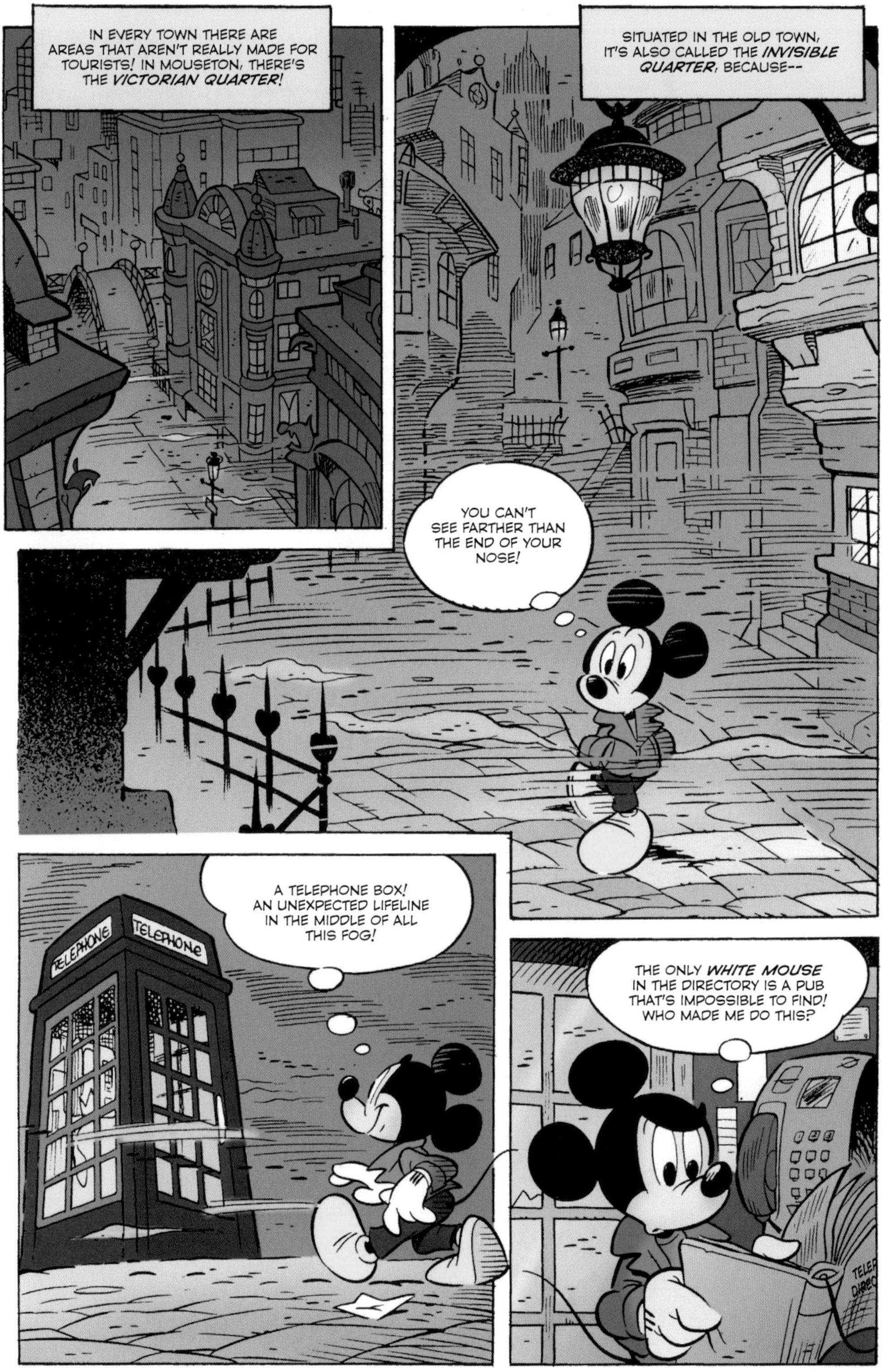
IN EVERY TOWN THERE ARE AREAS THAT AREN'T REALLY MADE FOR TOURISTS! IN MOUSETON, THERE'S THE VICTORIAN QUARTER!
SITUATED IN THE OLD TOWN, IT'S ALSO CALLED THE INVISIBLE QUARTER, BECAUSE--
YOU CAN'T SEE FARTHER THAN THE END OF YOUR NOSE!
A TELEPHONE BOX! AN UNEXPECTED LIFELINE IN THE MIDDLE OF ALL THIS FOG!
TELEPHONE
TELEPHONE
THE ONLY WHITE MOUSE IN THE DIRECTORY IS A PUB THAT'S IMPOSSIBLE TO FIND! WHO MADE ME DO THIS?

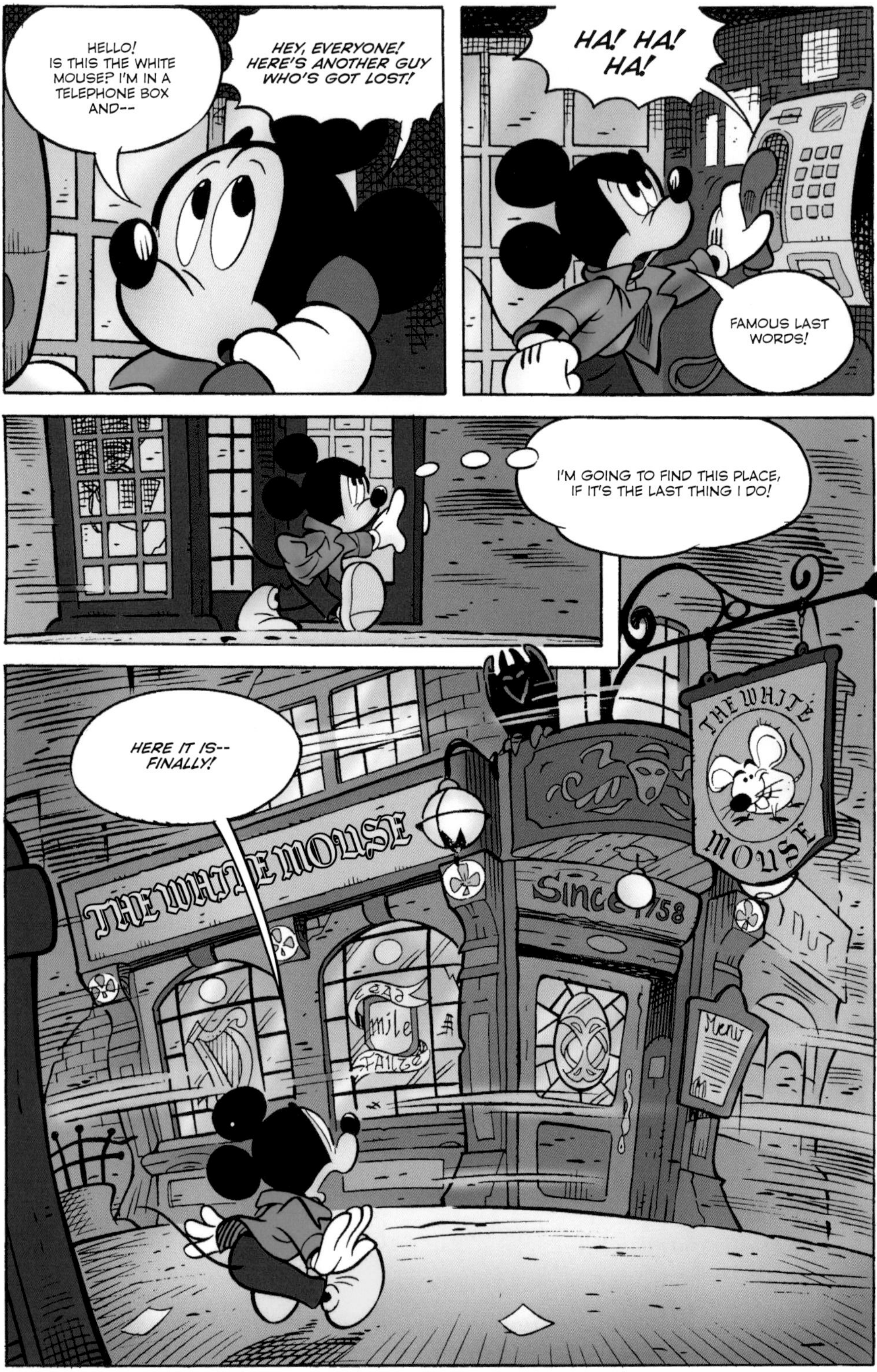
HELLO! IS THIS THE WHITE MOUSE? I'M IN A TELEPHONE BOX AND--
HEY, EVERYONE! HERE'S ANOTHER GUY WHO'S GOT LOST!
HA! HA! HA!
FAMOUS LAST WORDS!
I'M GOING TO FIND THIS PLACE, IF IT'S THE LAST THING I DO!
HERE IT IS-- FINALLY!
THE WHITE MOUSE
THE WHITE MOUSE
Since 1758
Menu

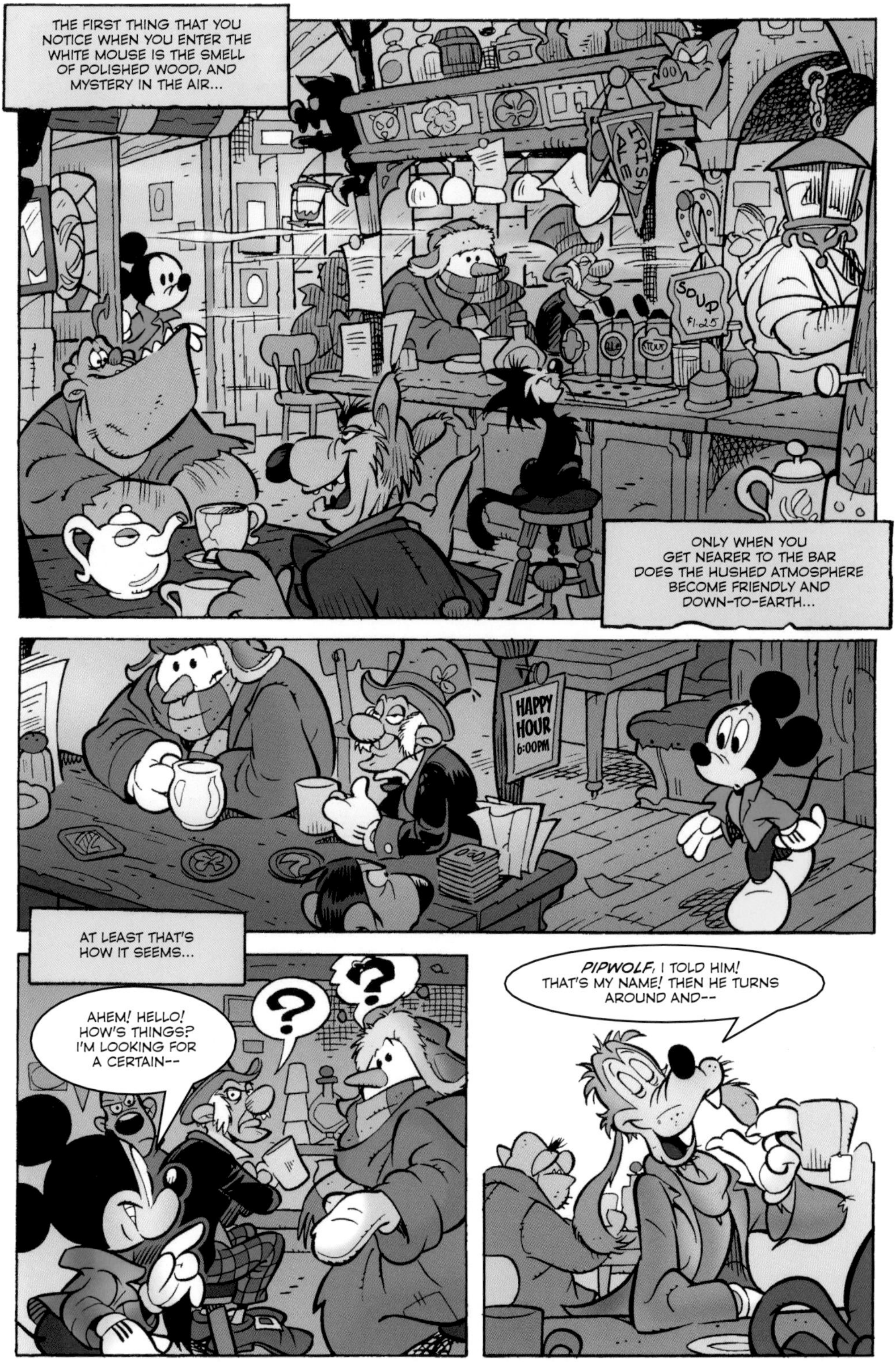
THE FIRST THING THAT YOU NOTICE WHEN YOU ENTER THE WHITE MOUSE IS THE SMELL OF POLISHED WOOD, AND MYSTERY IN THE AIR...
IRISH ALE
SOUP $1.25
ALE
STOUT
ONLY WHEN YOU GET NEARER TO THE BAR DOES THE HUSHED ATMOSPHERE BECOME FRIENDLY AND DOWN-TO-EARTH...
HAPPY HOUR 6:00PM
AT LEAST THAT'S HOW IT SEEMS...
AHEM! HELLO! HOW'S THINGS? I'M LOOKING FOR A CERTAIN--
?
?
*PIPWOLF*, I TOLD HIM! THAT'S MY NAME! THEN HE TURNS AROUND AND--

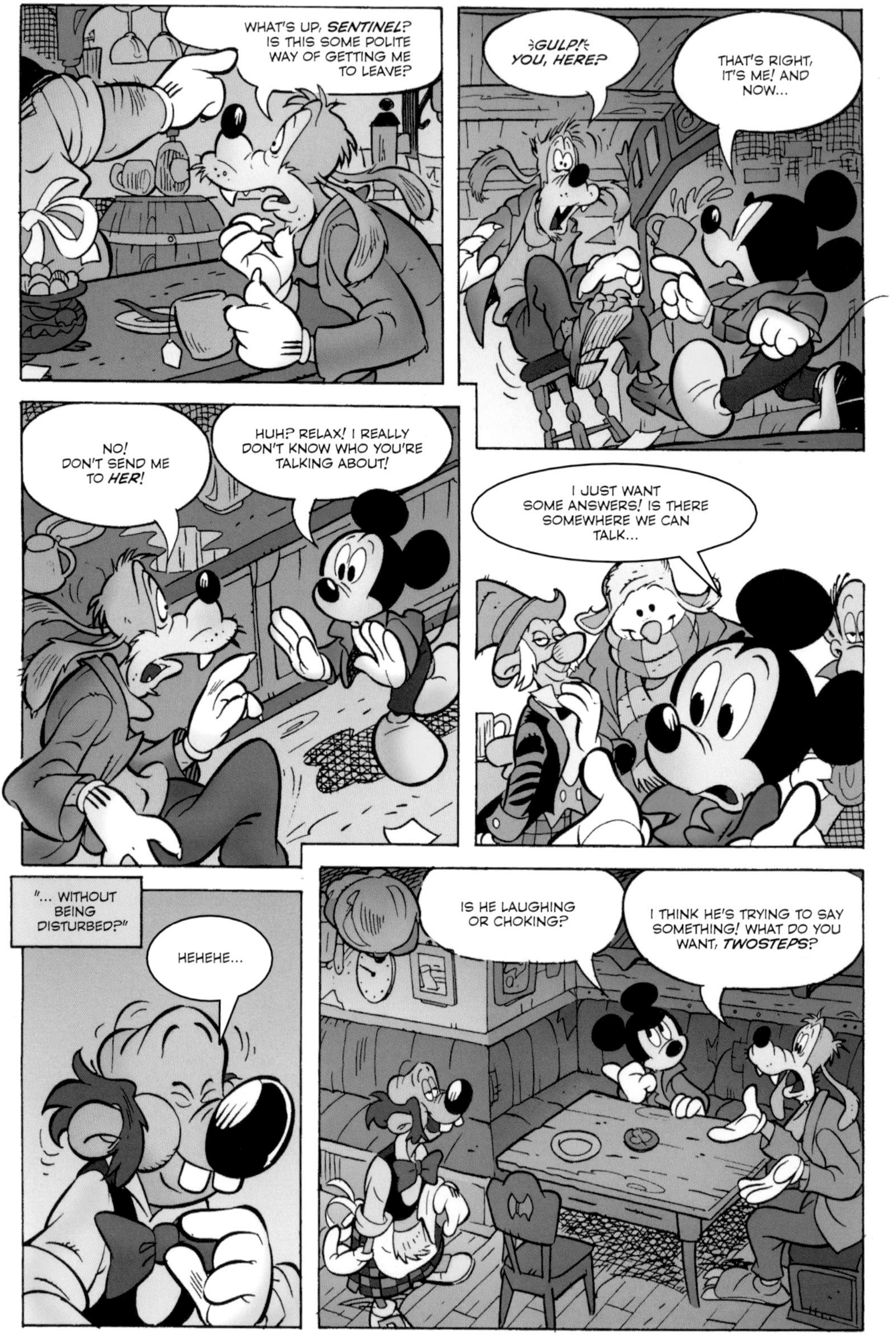
WHAT'S UP, SENTINEL? IS THIS SOME POLITE WAY OF GETTING ME TO LEAVE?
GULP! YOU, HERE?
THAT'S RIGHT, IT'S ME! AND NOW...
NO! DON'T SEND ME TO HER!
HUH? RELAX! I REALLY DON'T KNOW WHO YOU'RE TALKING ABOUT!
I JUST WANT SOME ANSWERS! IS THERE SOMEWHERE WE CAN TALK...
"... WITHOUT BEING DISTURBED?"
HEHEHE...
IS HE LAUGHING OR CHOKING?
I THINK HE'S TRYING TO SAY SOMETHING! WHAT DO YOU WANT, TWOSTEPS?

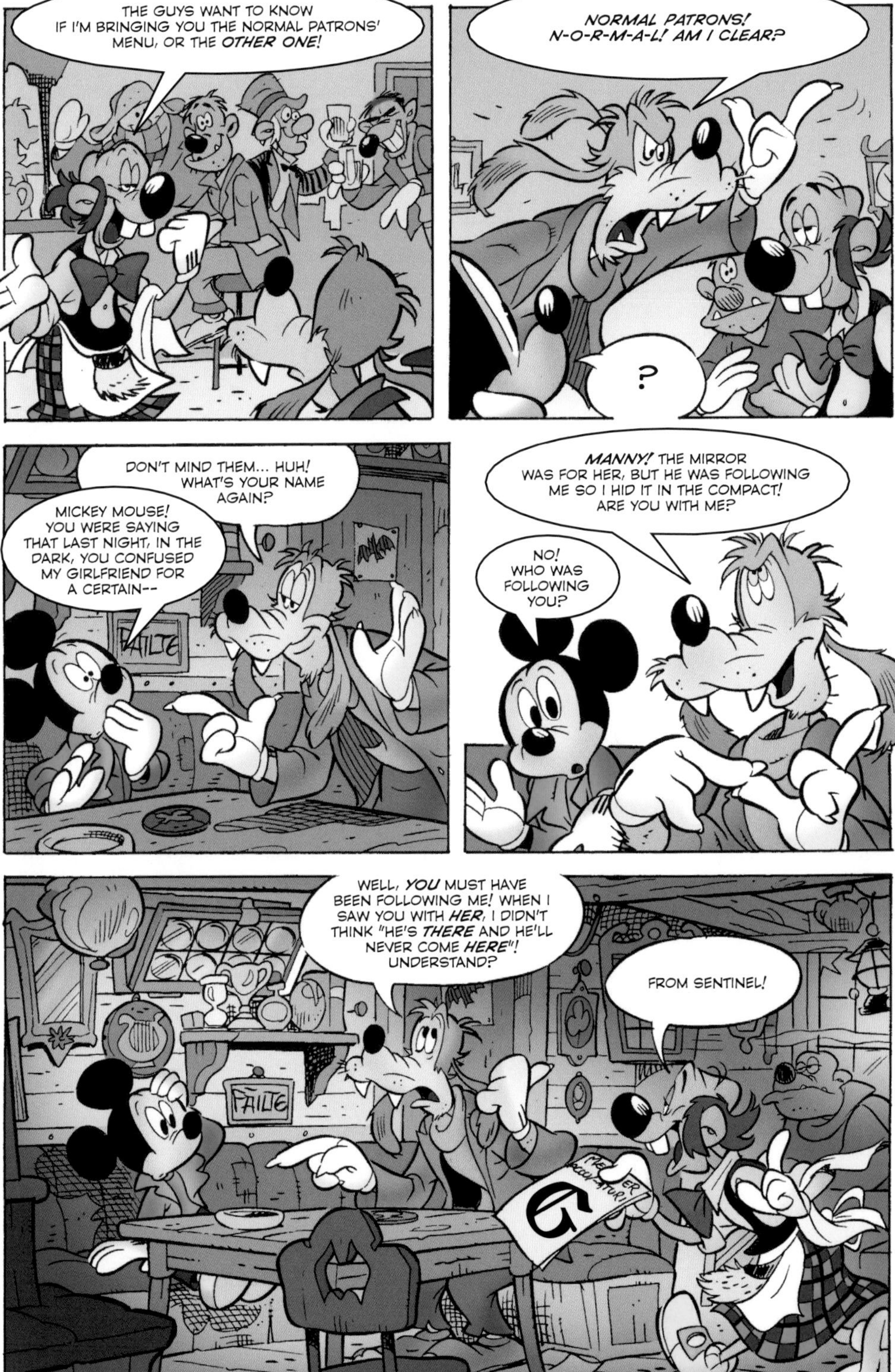
THE GUYS WANT TO KNOW IF I'M BRINGING YOU THE NORMAL PATRONS' MENU, OR THE *OTHER ONE!*
*NORMAL PATRONS! N-O-R-M-A-L! AM I CLEAR?*
?
DON'T MIND THEM... HUH! WHAT'S YOUR NAME AGAIN?
MICKEY MOUSE! YOU WERE SAYING THAT LAST NIGHT, IN THE DARK, YOU CONFUSED MY GIRLFRIEND FOR A CERTAIN--
FAILTE
*MANNY!* THE MIRROR WAS FOR HER, BUT HE WAS FOLLOWING ME SO I HID IT IN THE COMPACT! ARE YOU WITH ME?
NO! WHO WAS FOLLOWING YOU?
WELL, *YOU* MUST HAVE BEEN FOLLOWING ME! WHEN I SAW YOU WITH *HER*, I DIDN'T THINK "HE'S *THERE* AND HE'LL NEVER COME *HERE*"! UNDERSTAND?
FROM SENTINEL!
FAILTE

ARE YOU SURE, TWOSTEPS? DID SENTINEL TELL YOU TO GIVE US THE *OTHER* MENU?
HE KNEW STRAIGHT AWAY THAT YOUR GUEST WAS VERY *SPECIAL!*
MENU
G
*GUIDES'* MENU? WHAT DOES THAT MEAN?
THAT I'M DONE FOR! NOW EVERYONE'S GOING TO THINK YOU'RE--
GUIDES' MENU
G
*A TRAVELER!* ABOUT TIME TOO, PIPWOLF!
SMACK
HE SEEMS PRETTY SMART, TOO! EVEN THOUGH IT'S OBVIOUS HE'S NEVER TRAVELED!
GUIDES' MENU
G
HEY! I'VE SEEN PRACTICALLY THE WHOLE WORLD, MISTER!
WHAT DID I TELL YOU? HE'S ONLY SEEN *THIS* WORLD!
G
MICKEY! ALLOW ME TO INTRODUCE *HOBI* AND *MISTER SNOWMAN*, A.K.A. *ICE!*
BOO!
BOO!
BOO TO YOU, TOO! I NEARLY FORGOT THAT IN SOME PLACES PEOPLE GREET EACH OTHER LIKE THIS!

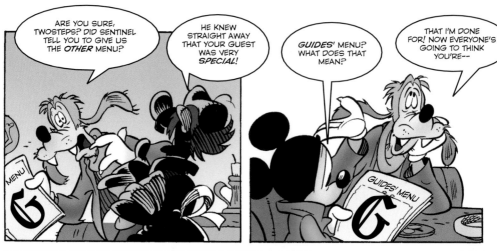

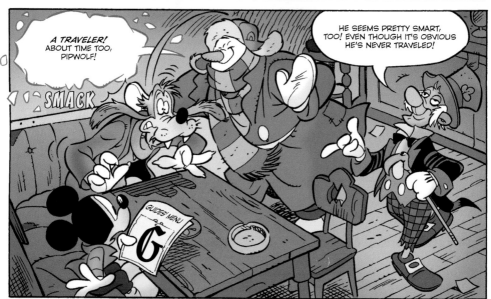

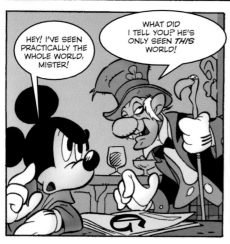

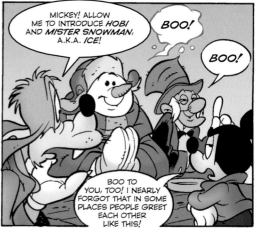

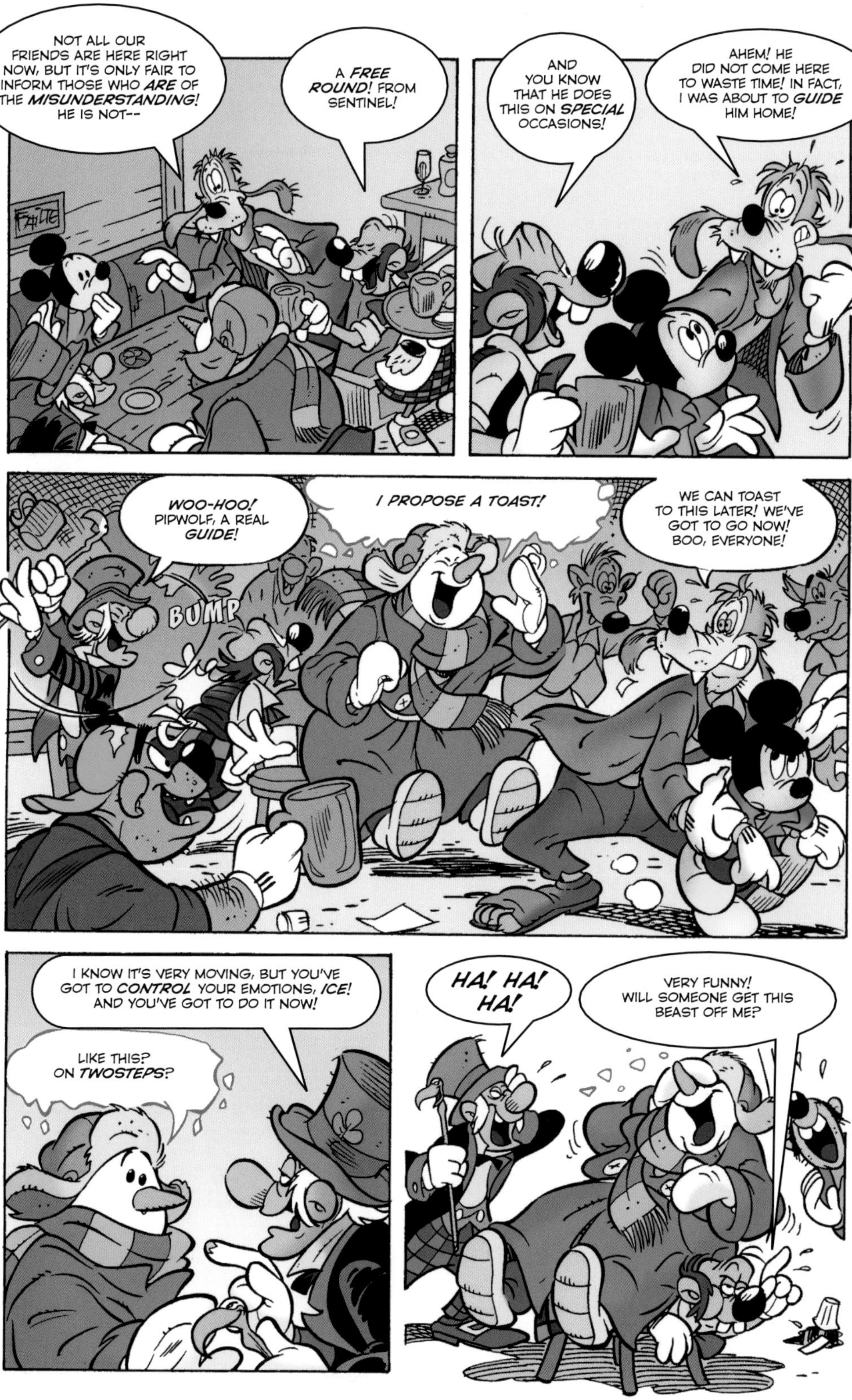
NOT ALL OUR FRIENDS ARE HERE RIGHT NOW, BUT IT'S ONLY FAIR TO INFORM THOSE WHO *ARE* OF THE *MISUNDERSTANDING!* HE IS NOT--
FÁILTE
A *FREE ROUND!* FROM SENTINEL!
AND YOU KNOW THAT HE DOES THIS ON *SPECIAL* OCCASIONS!
AHEM! HE DID NOT COME HERE TO WASTE TIME! IN FACT, I WAS ABOUT TO *GUIDE* HIM HOME!
*WOO-HOO!* PIPWOLF, A REAL *GUIDE!*
*I PROPOSE A TOAST!*
WE CAN TOAST TO THIS LATER! WE'VE GOT TO GO NOW! BOO, EVERYONE!
BUMP
I KNOW IT'S VERY MOVING, BUT YOU'VE GOT TO *CONTROL* YOUR EMOTIONS, *ICE!* AND YOU'VE GOT TO DO IT NOW!
LIKE THIS? ON *TWOSTEPS?*
*HA! HA! HA!*
VERY FUNNY! WILL SOMEONE GET THIS BEAST OFF ME?

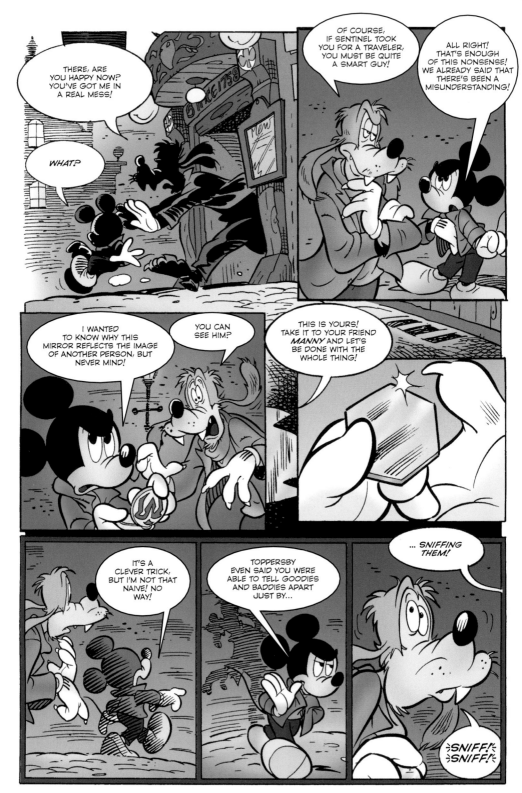

THERE, ARE YOU HAPPY NOW? YOU'VE GOT ME IN A REAL MESS!

WHAT?

OF COURSE, IF SENTINEL TOOK YOU FOR A TRAVELER, YOU MUST BE QUITE A SMART GUY!

ALL RIGHT! THAT'S ENOUGH OF THIS NONSENSE! WE ALREADY SAID THAT THERE'S BEEN A MISUNDERSTANDING!

I WANTED TO KNOW WHY THIS MIRROR REFLECTS THE IMAGE OF ANOTHER PERSON, BUT NEVER MIND!

YOU CAN SEE HIM?

THIS IS YOURS! TAKE IT TO YOUR FRIEND MANNY AND LET'S BE DONE WITH THE WHOLE THING!

IT'S A CLEVER TRICK, BUT I'M NOT THAT NAIVE! NO WAY!

TOPPERSBY EVEN SAID YOU WERE ABLE TO TELL GOODIES AND BADDIES APART JUST BY...

...SNIFFING THEM!

SNIFF! SNIFF!

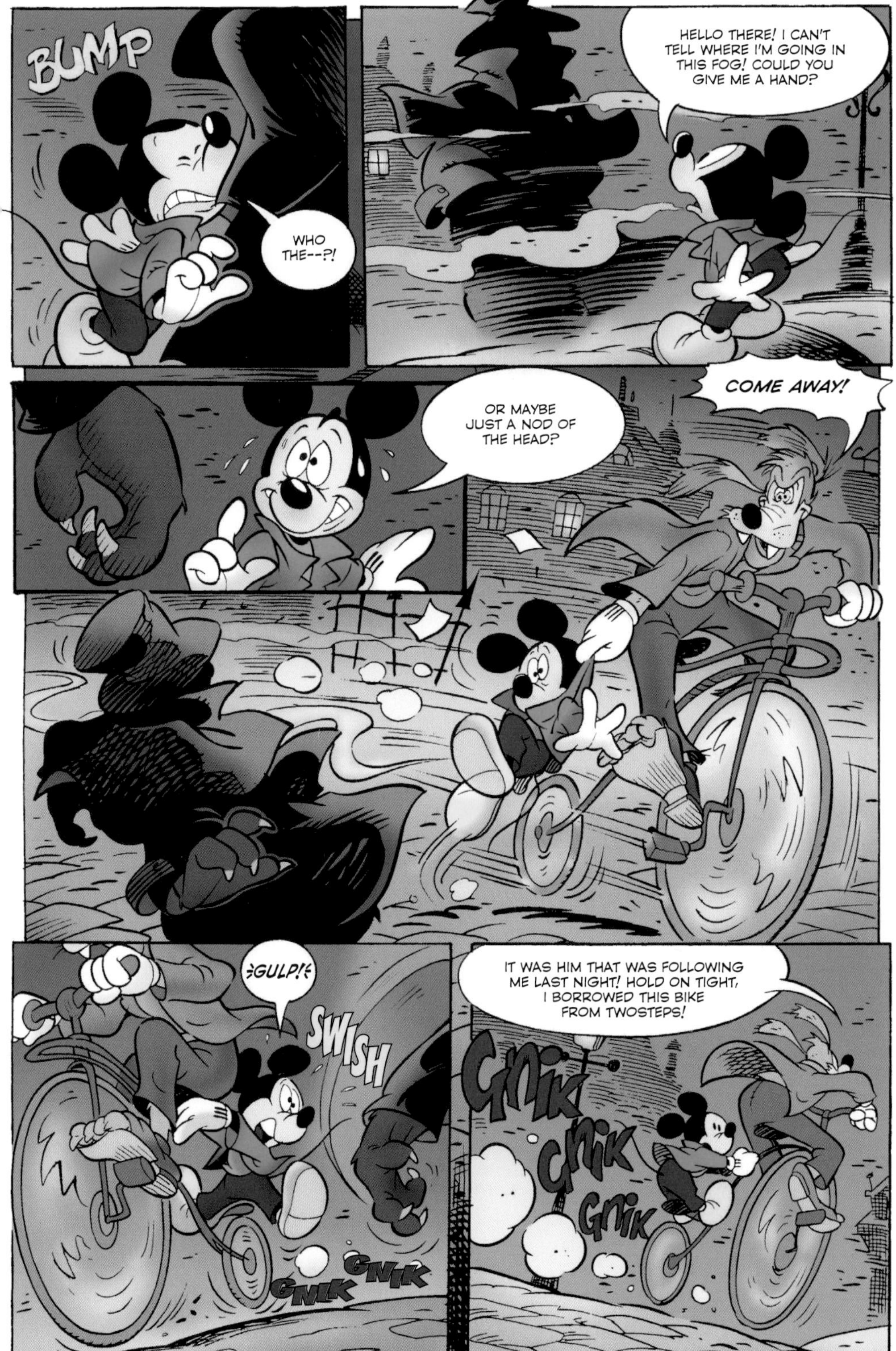

BUMP
WHO THE--?!
HELLO THERE! I CAN'T TELL WHERE I'M GOING IN THIS FOG! COULD YOU GIVE ME A HAND?
OR MAYBE JUST A NOD OF THE HEAD?
COME AWAY!
GULP!
SWISH
GNIK GNIK
IT WAS HIM THAT WAS FOLLOWING ME LAST NIGHT! HOLD ON TIGHT, I BORROWED THIS BIKE FROM TWOSTEPS!
GNIK GNIK GNIK

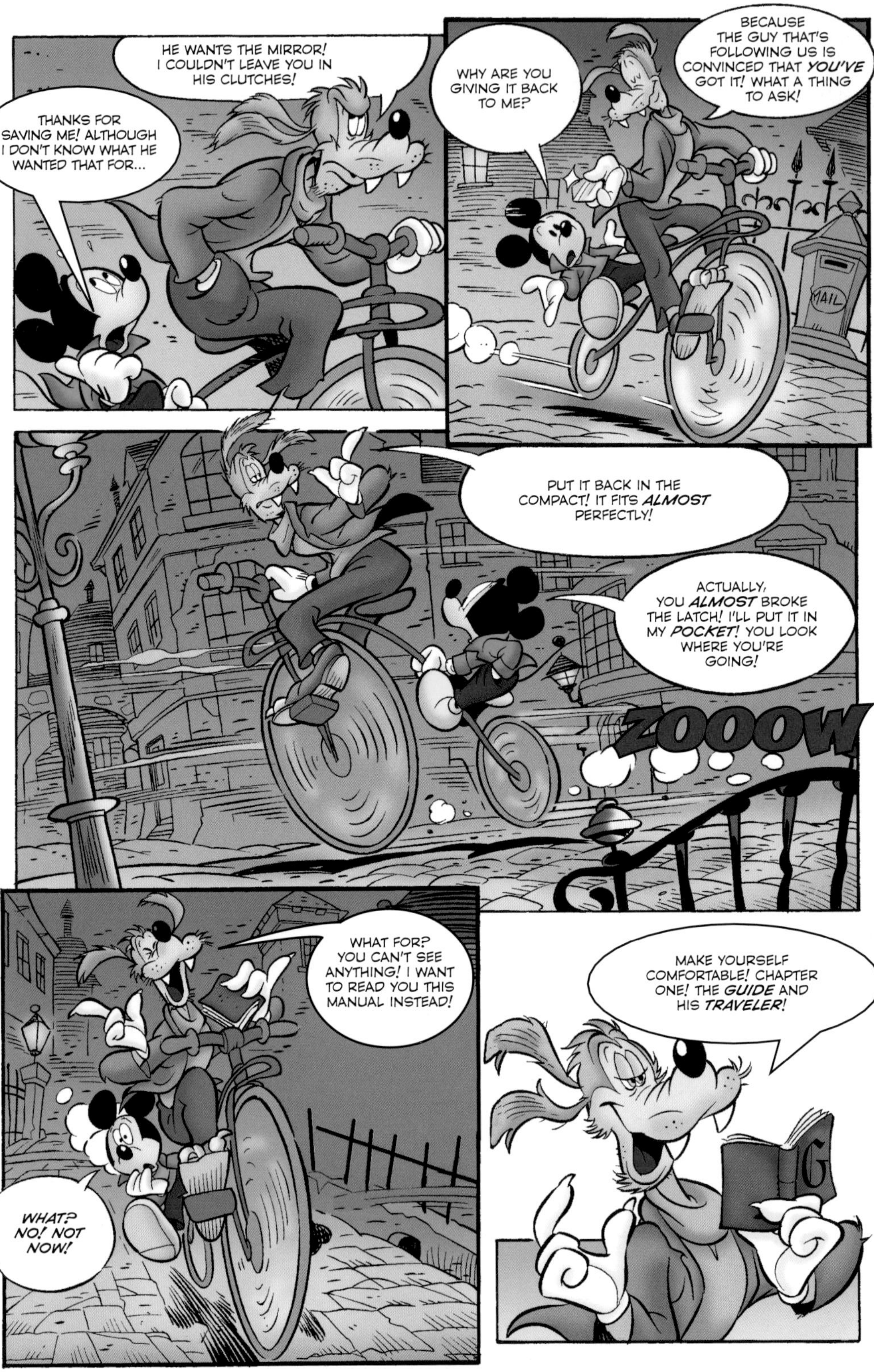
HE WANTS THE MIRROR! I COULDN'T LEAVE YOU IN HIS CLUTCHES!
THANKS FOR SAVING ME! ALTHOUGH I DON'T KNOW WHAT HE WANTED THAT FOR...
WHY ARE YOU GIVING IT BACK TO ME?
BECAUSE THE GUY THAT'S FOLLOWING US IS CONVINCED THAT YOU'VE GOT IT! WHAT A THING TO ASK!
MAIL
PUT IT BACK IN THE COMPACT! IT FITS ALMOST PERFECTLY!
ACTUALLY, YOU ALMOST BROKE THE LATCH! I'LL PUT IT IN MY POCKET! YOU LOOK WHERE YOU'RE GOING!
ZOOOW
WHAT FOR? YOU CAN'T SEE ANYTHING! I WANT TO READ YOU THIS MANUAL INSTEAD!
WHAT? NO! NOT NOW!
MAKE YOURSELF COMFORTABLE! CHAPTER ONE! THE GUIDE AND HIS TRAVELER!
G

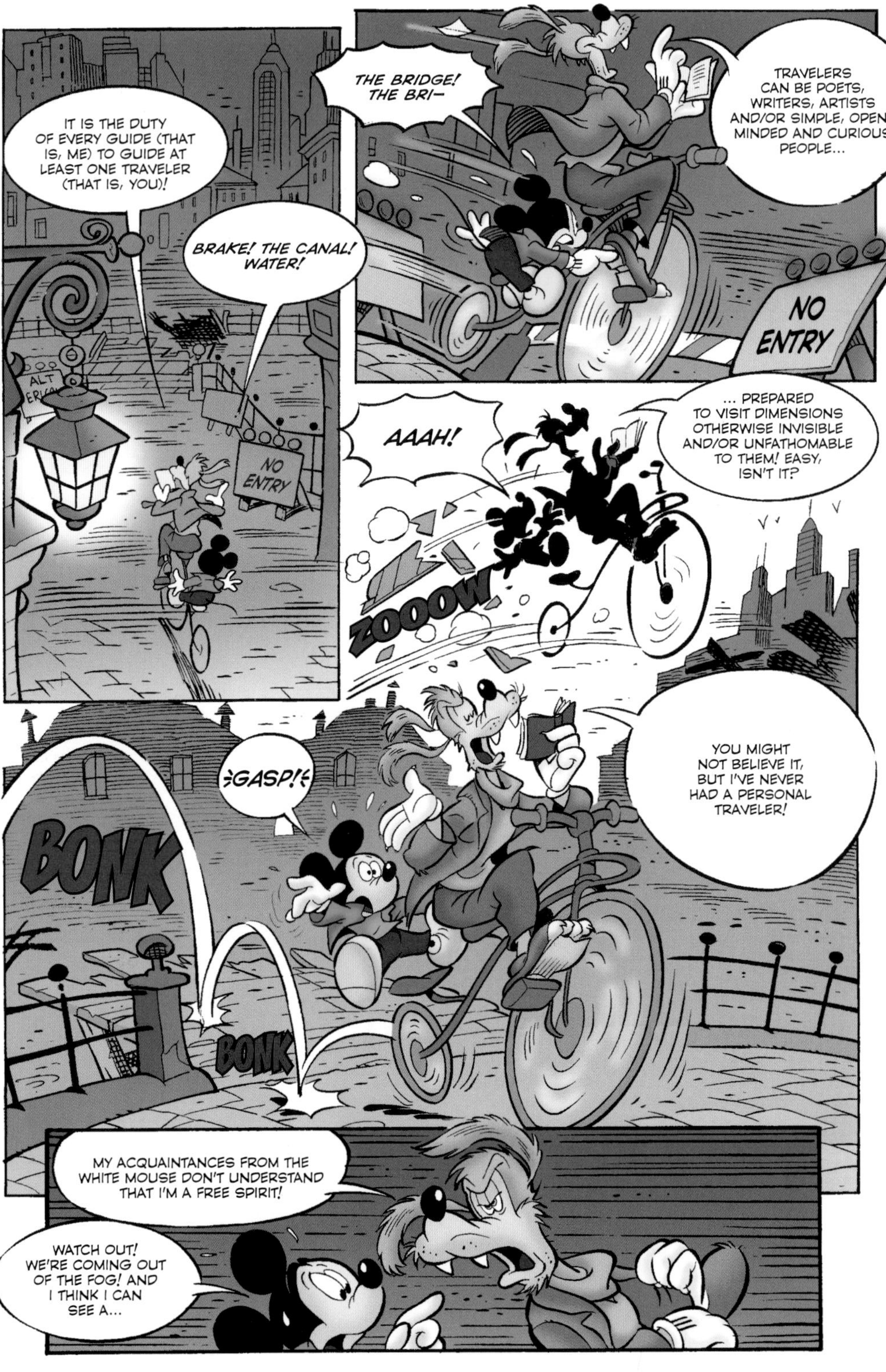

IT IS THE DUTY OF EVERY GUIDE (THAT IS, ME) TO GUIDE AT LEAST ONE TRAVELER (THAT IS, YOU)!
BRAKE! THE CANAL! WATER!
NO ENTRY
THE BRIDGE! THE BRI—
TRAVELERS CAN BE POETS, WRITERS, ARTISTS AND/OR SIMPLE, OPEN-MINDED AND CURIOUS PEOPLE...
NO ENTRY
AAAH!
... PREPARED TO VISIT DIMENSIONS OTHERWISE INVISIBLE AND/OR UNFATHOMABLE TO THEM! EASY, ISN'T IT?
ZOOOW
BONK
GASP!
YOU MIGHT NOT BELIEVE IT, BUT I'VE NEVER HAD A PERSONAL TRAVELER!
BONK
MY ACQUAINTANCES FROM THE WHITE MOUSE DON'T UNDERSTAND THAT I'M A FREE SPIRIT!
WATCH OUT! WE'RE COMING OUT OF THE FOG! AND I THINK I CAN SEE A...

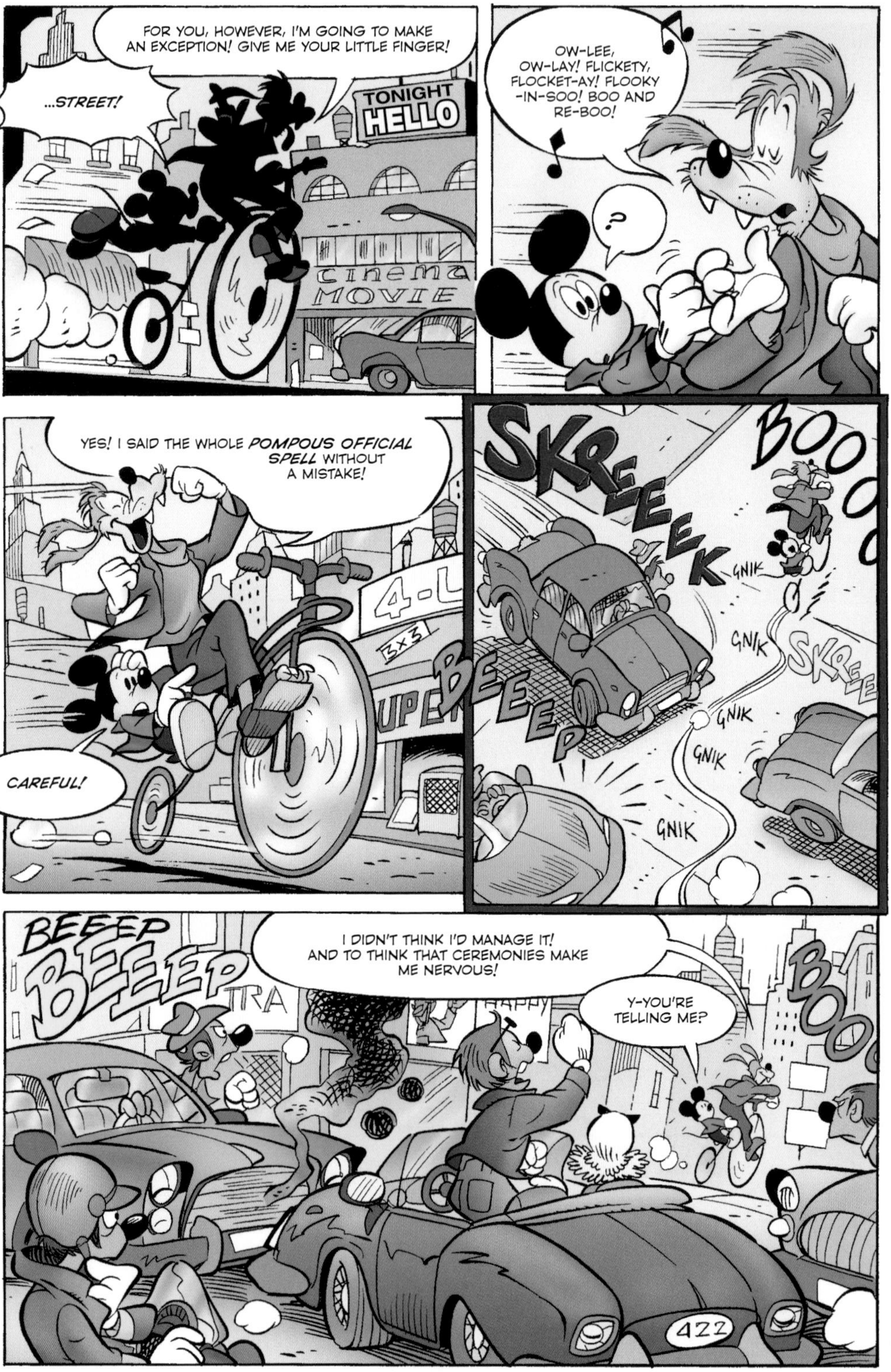
...STREET!
FOR YOU, HOWEVER, I'M GOING TO MAKE AN EXCEPTION! GIVE ME YOUR LITTLE FINGER!
TONIGHT HELLO
cinema MOVIE
OW-LEE, OW-LAY! FLICKETY, FLOCKET-AY! FLOOKY -IN-SOO! BOO AND RE-BOO!
?
YES! I SAID THE WHOLE *POMPOUS OFFICIAL SPELL* WITHOUT A MISTAKE!
CAREFUL!
3x3
BEEEEP
SKREEEEK
BOOOO
GNIK
GNIK
GNIK
GNIK
GNIK
BEEEP
BEEEP
I DIDN'T THINK I'D MANAGE IT! AND TO THINK THAT CEREMONIES MAKE ME NERVOUS!
Y-YOU'RE TELLING ME?
422

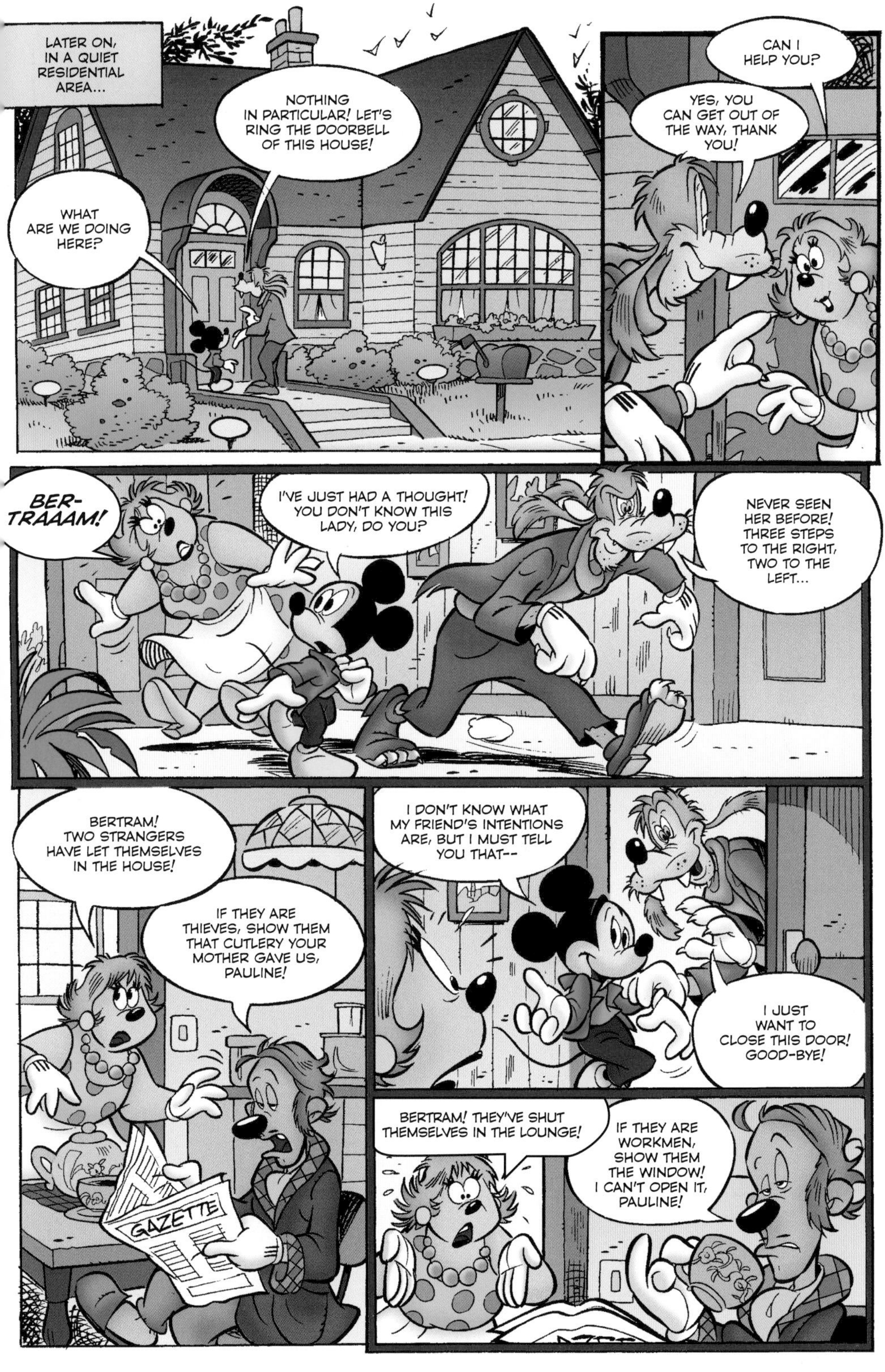
LATER ON, IN A QUIET RESIDENTIAL AREA...
WHAT ARE WE DOING HERE?
NOTHING IN PARTICULAR! LET'S RING THE DOORBELL OF THIS HOUSE!
CAN I HELP YOU?
YES, YOU CAN GET OUT OF THE WAY, THANK YOU!
BER-TRAAAM!
I'VE JUST HAD A THOUGHT! YOU DON'T KNOW THIS LADY, DO YOU?
NEVER SEEN HER BEFORE! THREE STEPS TO THE RIGHT, TWO TO THE LEFT...
BERTRAM! TWO STRANGERS HAVE LET THEMSELVES IN THE HOUSE!
IF THEY ARE THIEVES, SHOW THEM THAT CUTLERY YOUR MOTHER GAVE US, PAULINE!
GAZETTE
I DON'T KNOW WHAT MY FRIEND'S INTENTIONS ARE, BUT I MUST TELL YOU THAT--
I JUST WANT TO CLOSE THIS DOOR! GOOD-BYE!
BERTRAM! THEY'VE SHUT THEMSELVES IN THE LOUNGE!
IF THEY ARE WORKMEN, SHOW THEM THE WINDOW! I CAN'T OPEN IT, PAULINE!

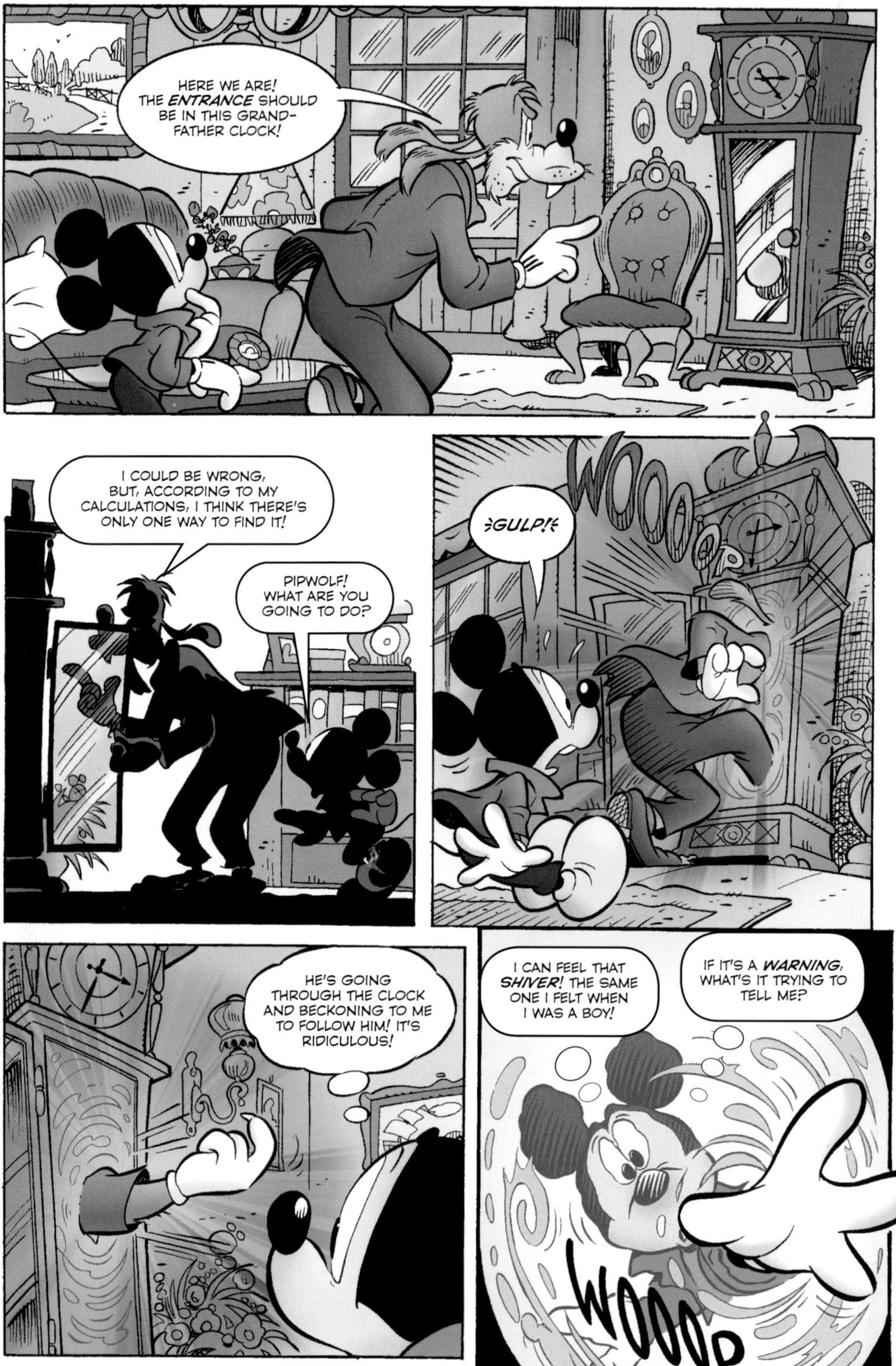
HERE WE ARE! THE ENTRANCE SHOULD BE IN THIS GRAND-FATHER CLOCK!
I COULD BE WRONG, BUT, ACCORDING TO MY CALCULATIONS, I THINK THERE'S ONLY ONE WAY TO FIND IT!
PIPWOLF! WHAT ARE YOU GOING TO DO?
WOOOOOP
GULP!
HE'S GOING THROUGH THE CLOCK AND BECKONING TO ME TO FOLLOW HIM! IT'S RIDICULOUS!
I CAN FEEL THAT SHIVER! THE SAME ONE I FELT WHEN I WAS A BOY!
IF IT'S A WARNING, WHAT'S IT TRYING TO TELL ME?
WOOOP

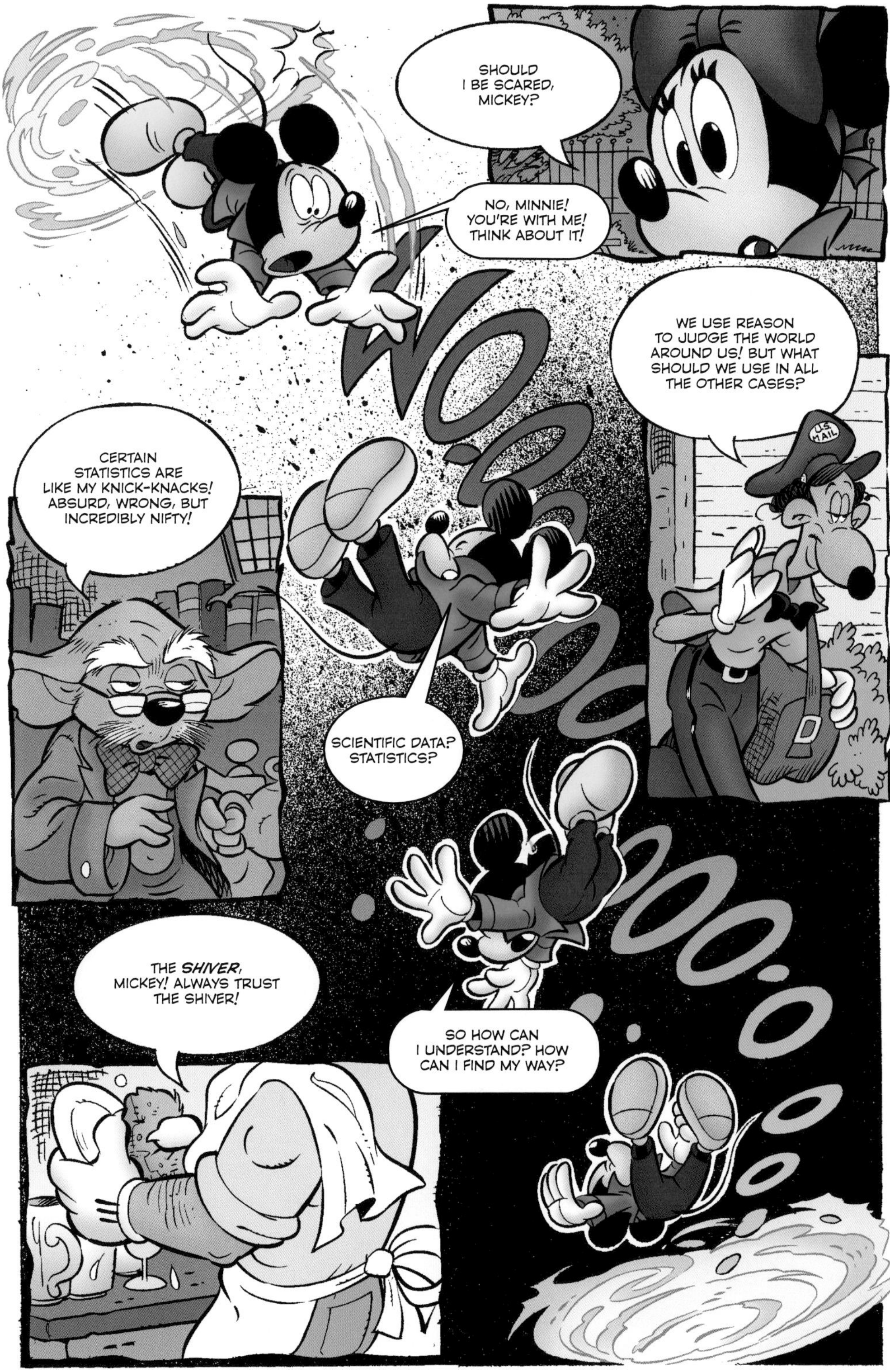
SHOULD I BE SCARED, MICKEY?
NO, MINNIE! YOU'RE WITH ME! THINK ABOUT IT!
WE USE REASON TO JUDGE THE WORLD AROUND US! BUT WHAT SHOULD WE USE IN ALL THE OTHER CASES?
CERTAIN STATISTICS ARE LIKE MY KNICK-KNACKS! ABSURD, WRONG, BUT INCREDIBLY NIFTY!
SCIENTIFIC DATA? STATISTICS?
U.S. MAIL
THE SHIVER, MICKEY! ALWAYS TRUST THE SHIVER!
SO HOW CAN I UNDERSTAND? HOW CAN I FIND MY WAY?

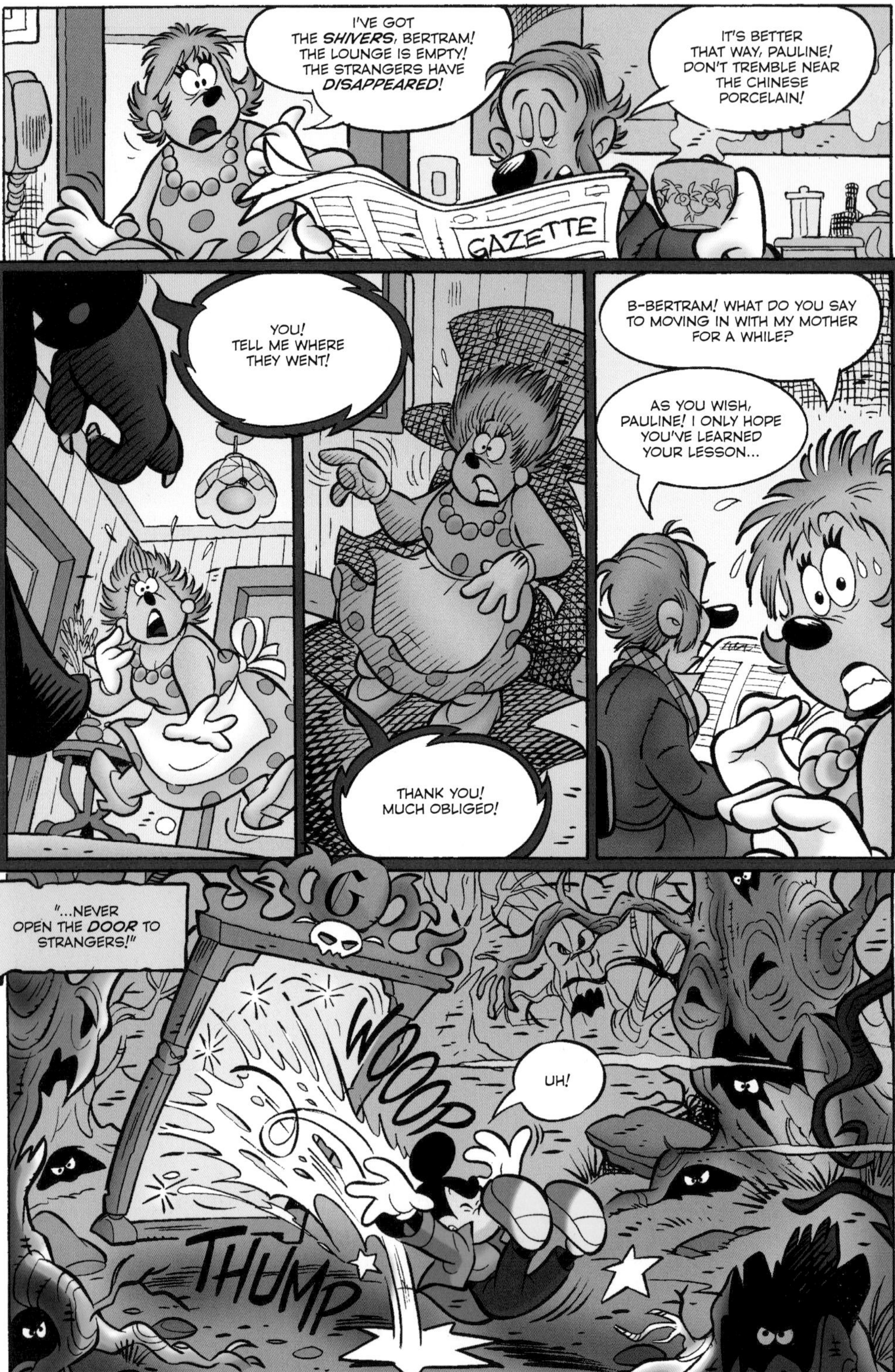
I'VE GOT THE SHIVERS, BERTRAM! THE LOUNGE IS EMPTY! THE STRANGERS HAVE DISAPPEARED!
IT'S BETTER THAT WAY, PAULINE! DON'T TREMBLE NEAR THE CHINESE PORCELAIN!
GAZETTE
YOU! TELL ME WHERE THEY WENT!
THANK YOU! MUCH OBLIGED!
B-BERTRAM! WHAT DO YOU SAY TO MOVING IN WITH MY MOTHER FOR A WHILE?
AS YOU WISH, PAULINE! I ONLY HOPE YOU'VE LEARNED YOUR LESSON...
"...NEVER OPEN THE DOOR TO STRANGERS!"
G
WOOOP
UH!
THUMP

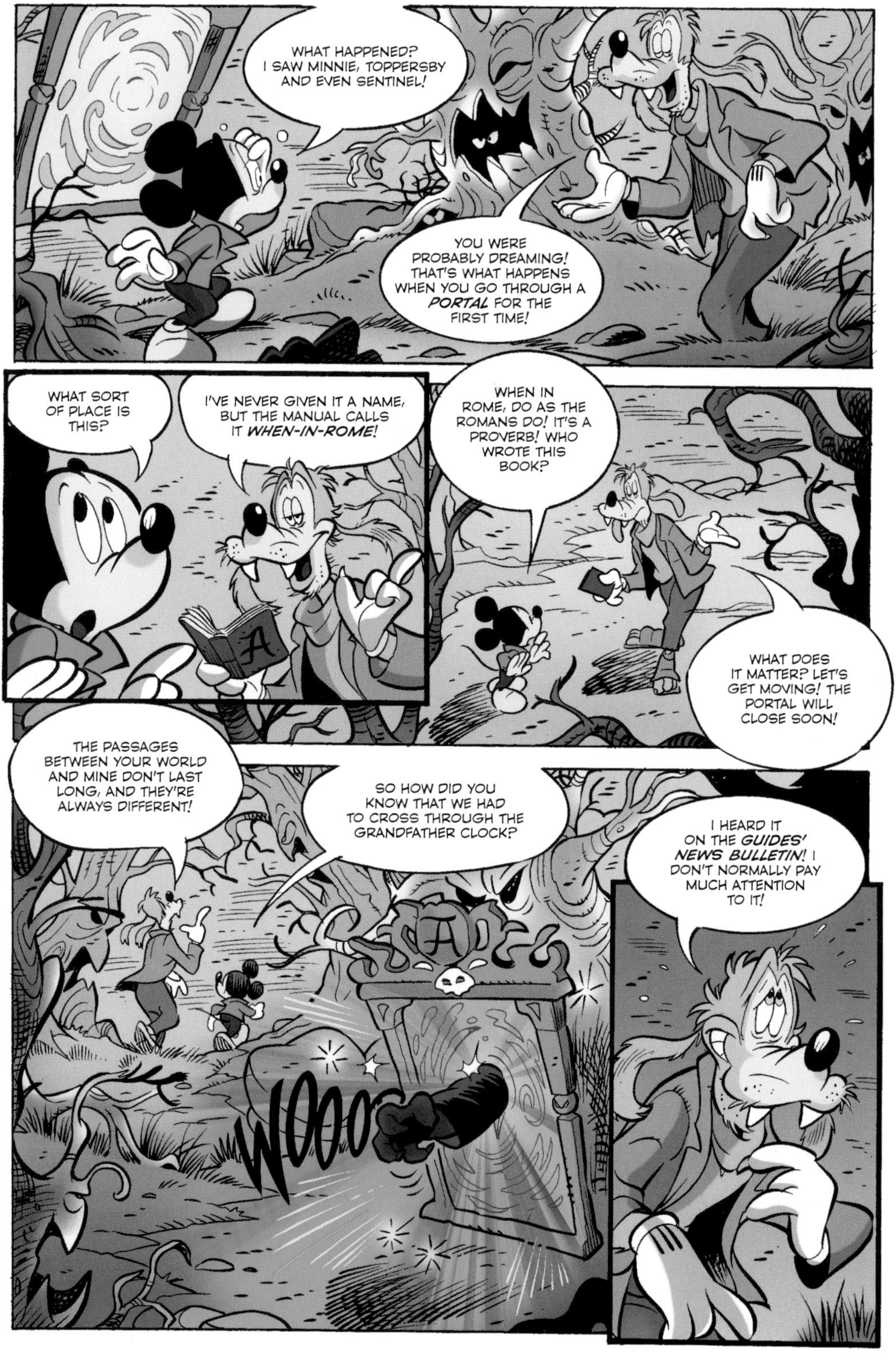
WHAT HAPPENED? I SAW MINNIE, TOPPERSBY AND EVEN SENTINEL!
YOU WERE PROBABLY DREAMING! THAT'S WHAT HAPPENS WHEN YOU GO THROUGH A PORTAL FOR THE FIRST TIME!
WHAT SORT OF PLACE IS THIS?
I'VE NEVER GIVEN IT A NAME, BUT THE MANUAL CALLS IT WHEN-IN-ROME!
WHEN IN ROME, DO AS THE ROMANS DO! IT'S A PROVERB! WHO WROTE THIS BOOK?
WHAT DOES IT MATTER? LET'S GET MOVING! THE PORTAL WILL CLOSE SOON!
THE PASSAGES BETWEEN YOUR WORLD AND MINE DON'T LAST LONG, AND THEY'RE ALWAYS DIFFERENT!
SO HOW DID YOU KNOW THAT WE HAD TO CROSS THROUGH THE GRANDFATHER CLOCK?
WOOOO
I HEARD IT ON THE GUIDES' NEWS BULLETIN! I DON'T NORMALLY PAY MUCH ATTENTION TO IT!

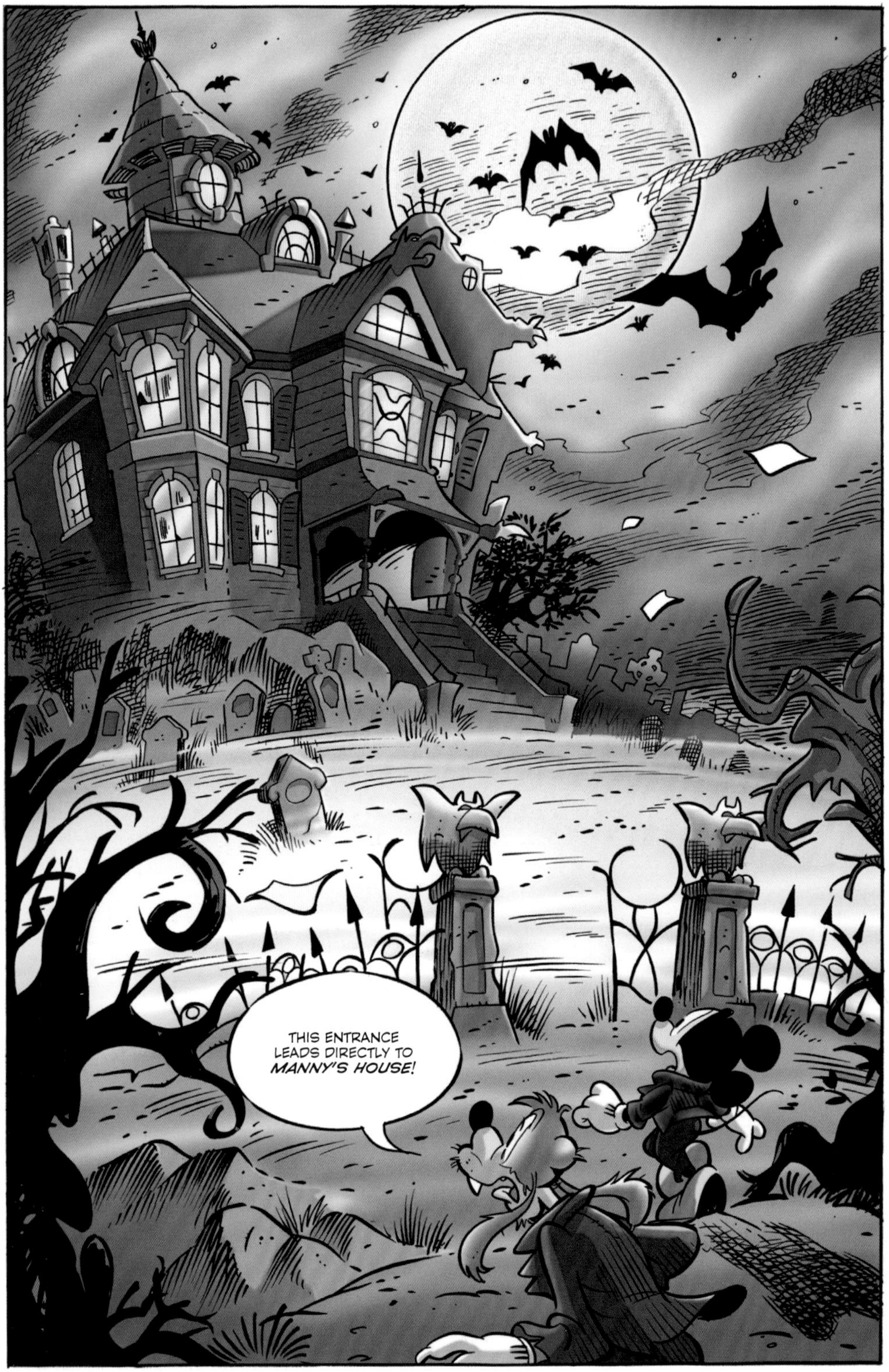
THIS ENTRANCE LEADS DIRECTLY TO MANNY'S HOUSE!

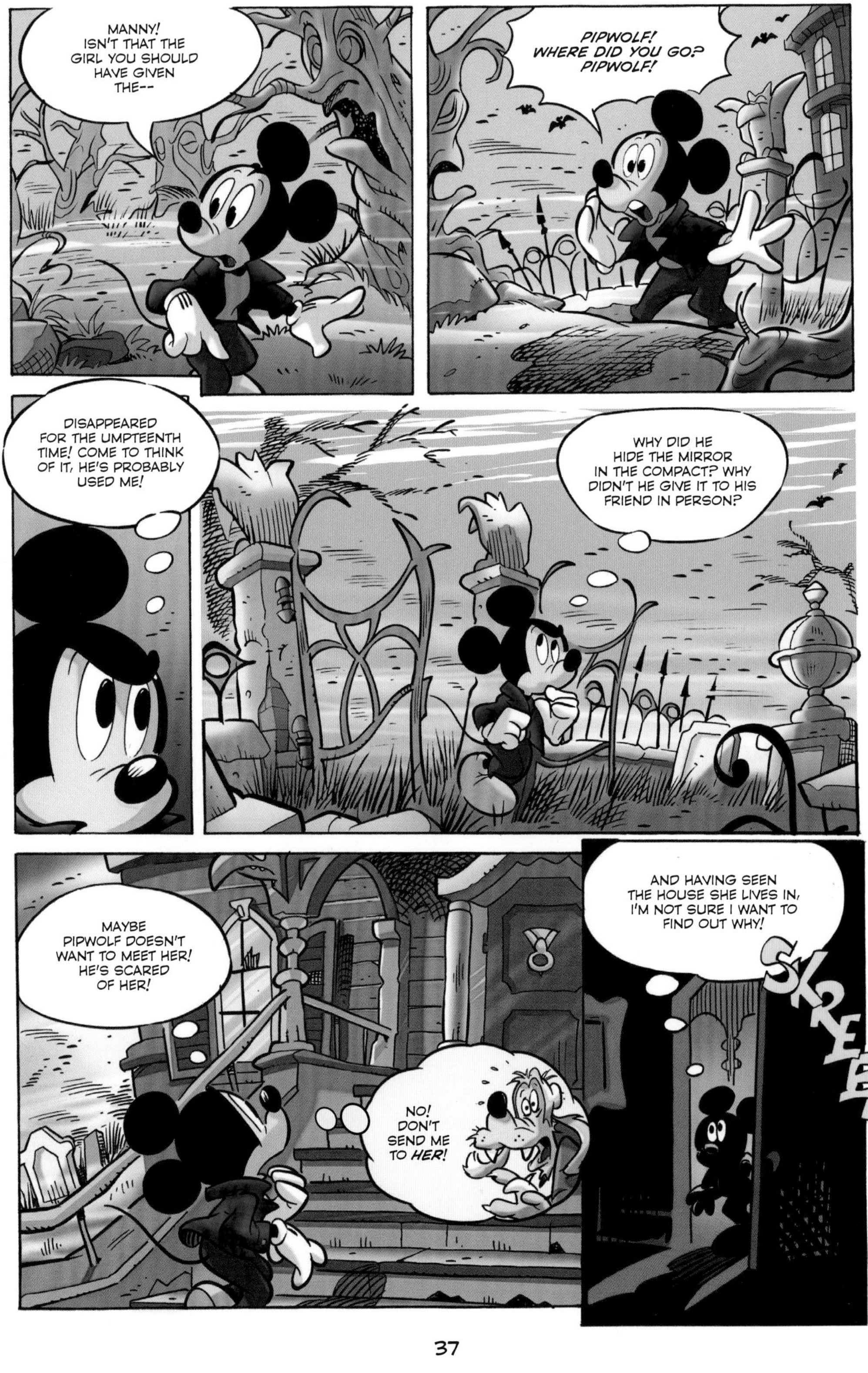
MANNY! ISN'T THAT THE GIRL YOU SHOULD HAVE GIVEN THE--
PIPWOLF! WHERE DID YOU GO? PIPWOLF!
DISAPPEARED FOR THE UMPTEENTH TIME! COME TO THINK OF IT, HE'S PROBABLY USED ME!
WHY DID HE HIDE THE MIRROR IN THE COMPACT? WHY DIDN'T HE GIVE IT TO HIS FRIEND IN PERSON?
MAYBE PIPWOLF DOESN'T WANT TO MEET HER! HE'S SCARED OF HER!
NO! DON'T SEND ME TO *HER*!
AND HAVING SEEN THE HOUSE SHE LIVES IN, I'M NOT SURE I WANT TO FIND OUT WHY!
SKREEK

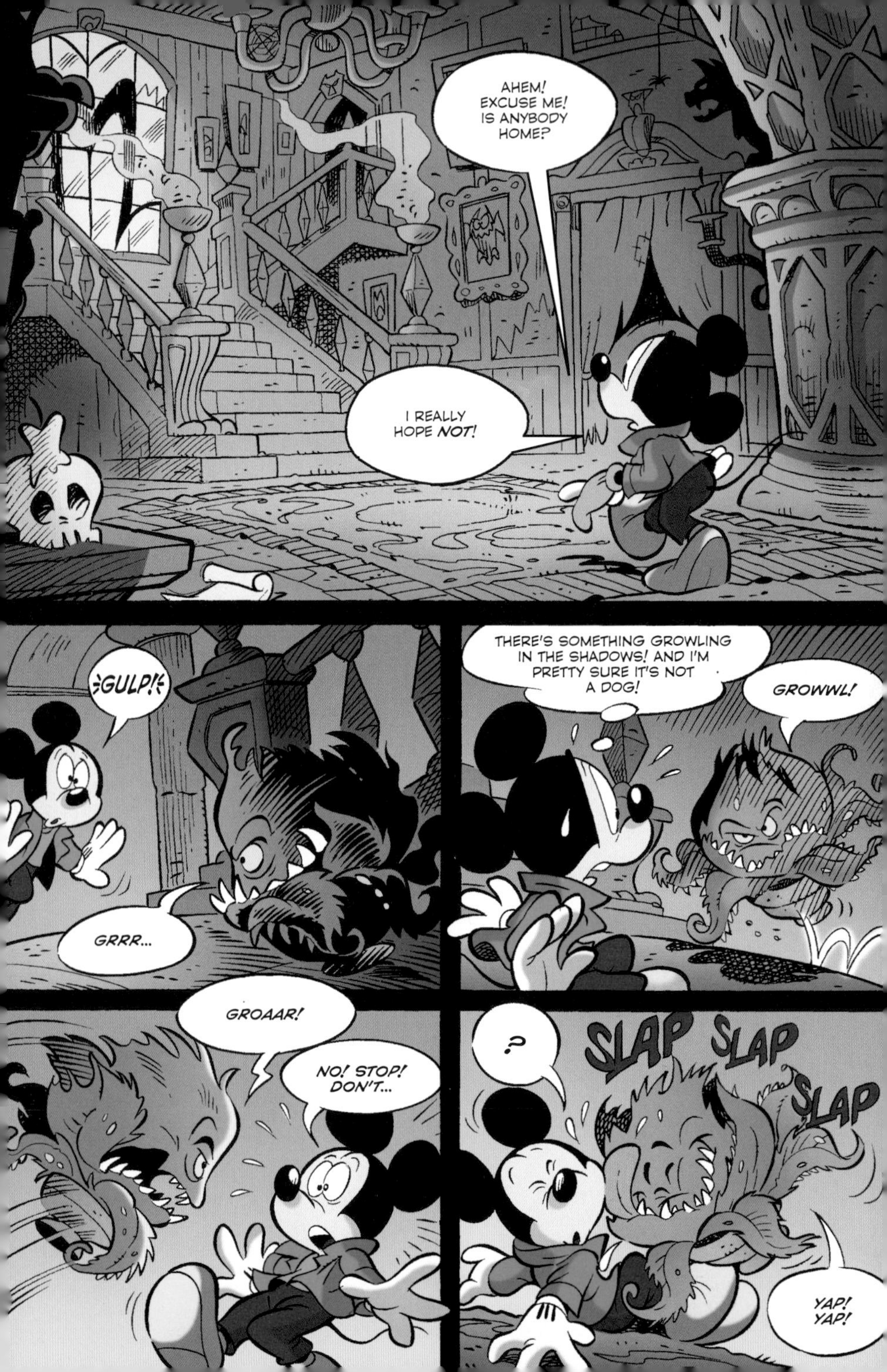

AHEM! EXCUSE ME! IS ANYBODY HOME?
I REALLY HOPE NOT!
GULP!
GRRR...
THERE'S SOMETHING GROWLING IN THE SHADOWS! AND I'M PRETTY SURE IT'S NOT A DOG!
GROWWL!
GROAAR!
NO! STOP! DON'T...
?
SLAP SLAP SLAP
YAP! YAP!

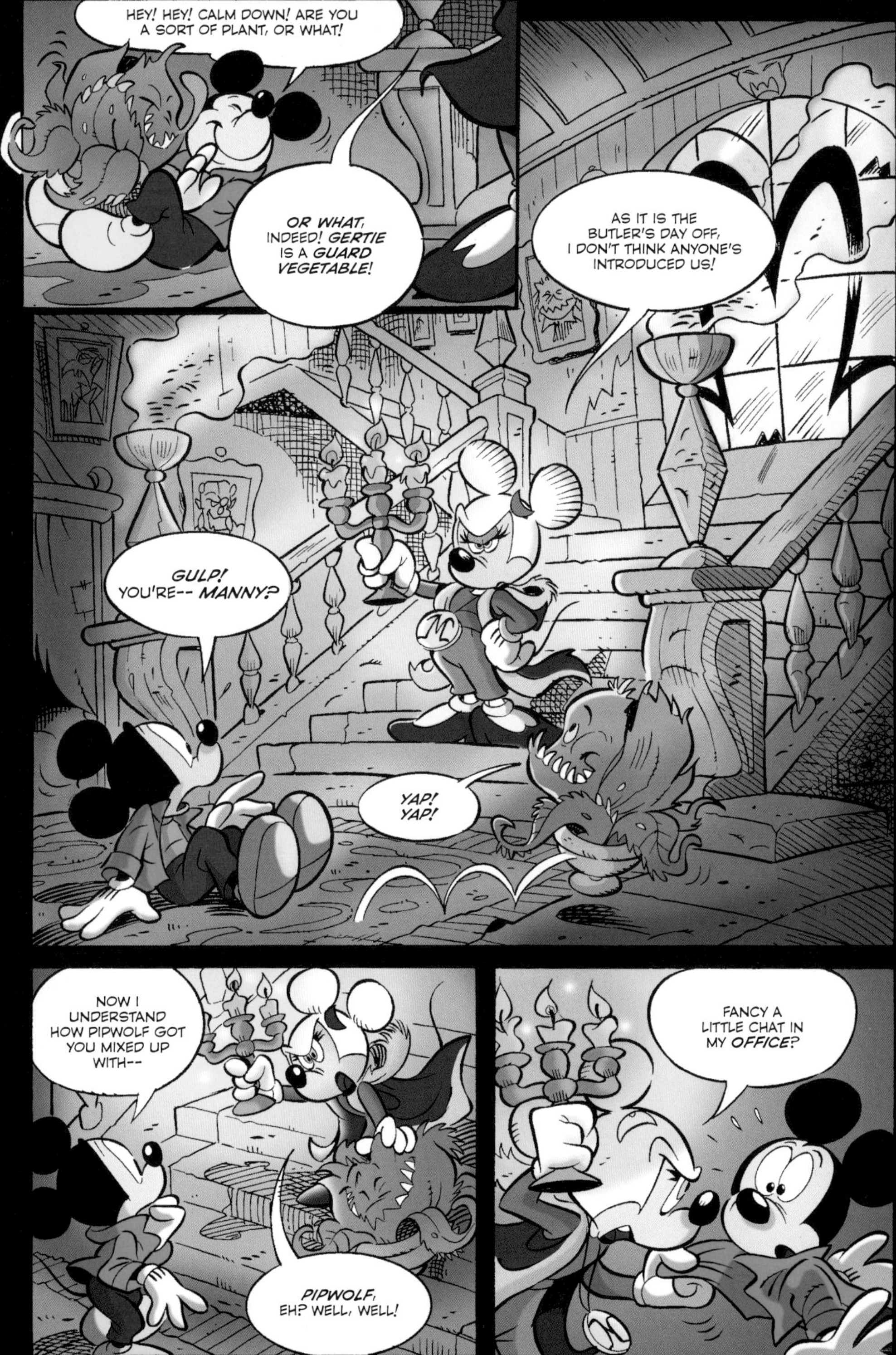
HEY! HEY! CALM DOWN! ARE YOU A SORT OF PLANT, OR WHAT!
OR WHAT, INDEED! GERTIE IS A GUARD VEGETABLE!
AS IT IS THE BUTLER'S DAY OFF, I DON'T THINK ANYONE'S INTRODUCED US!
GULP! YOU'RE-- MANNY?
YAP! YAP!
NOW I UNDERSTAND HOW PIPWOLF GOT YOU MIXED UP WITH--
PIPWOLF, EH? WELL, WELL!
FANCY A LITTLE CHAT IN MY OFFICE?

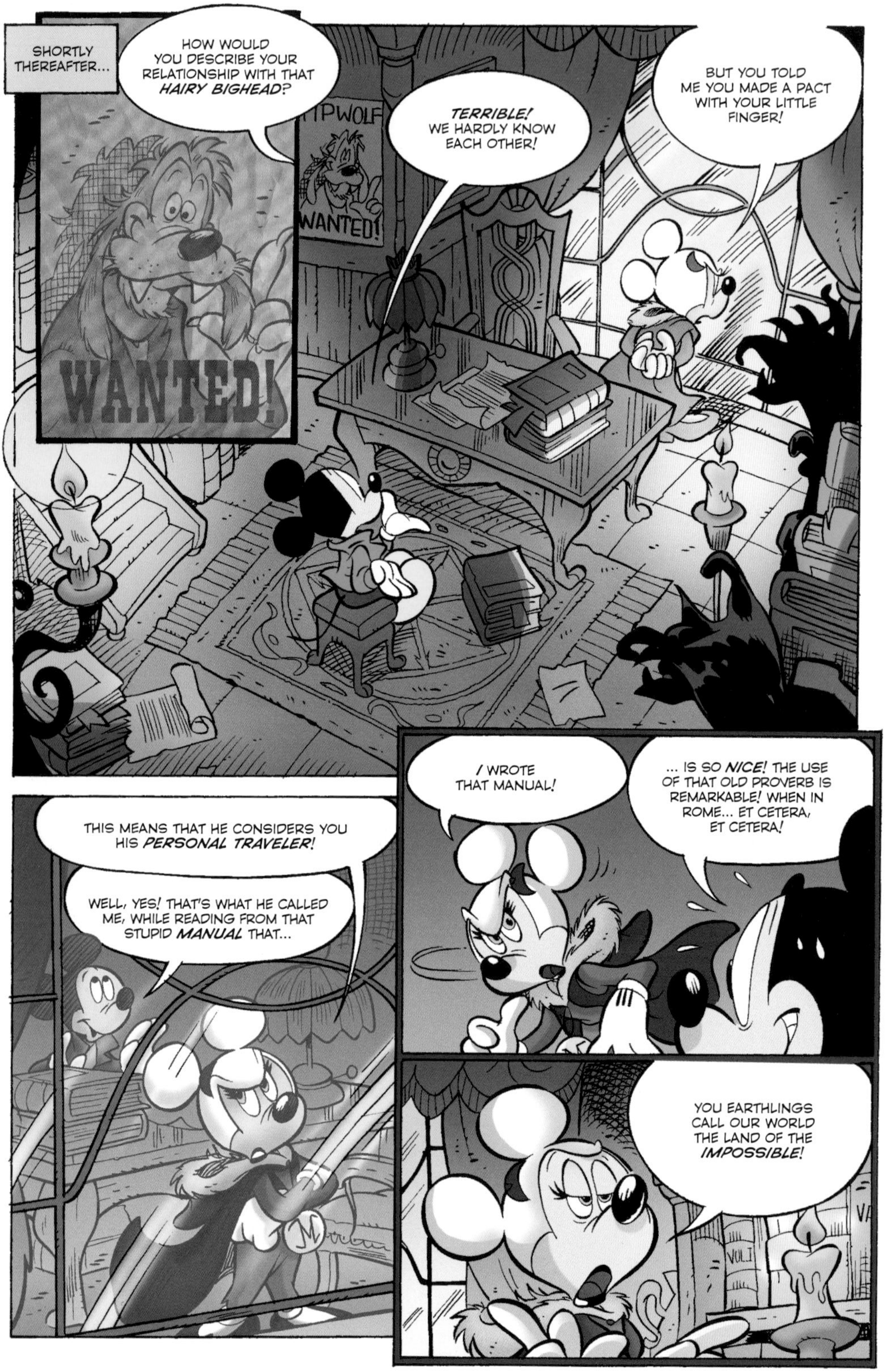
SHORTLY THEREAFTER...
HOW WOULD YOU DESCRIBE YOUR RELATIONSHIP WITH THAT *HAIRY BIGHEAD*?
WANTED!
*TERRIBLE!* WE HARDLY KNOW EACH OTHER!
BUT YOU TOLD ME YOU MADE A PACT WITH YOUR LITTLE FINGER!
THIS MEANS THAT HE CONSIDERS YOU HIS *PERSONAL TRAVELER!*
WELL, YES! THAT'S WHAT HE CALLED ME, WHILE READING FROM THAT STUPID *MANUAL* THAT...
*I* WROTE THAT MANUAL!
... IS SO *NICE!* THE USE OF THAT OLD PROVERB IS REMARKABLE! WHEN IN ROME... ET CETERA, ET CETERA!
YOU EARTHLINGS CALL OUR WORLD THE LAND OF THE *IMPOSSIBLE!*

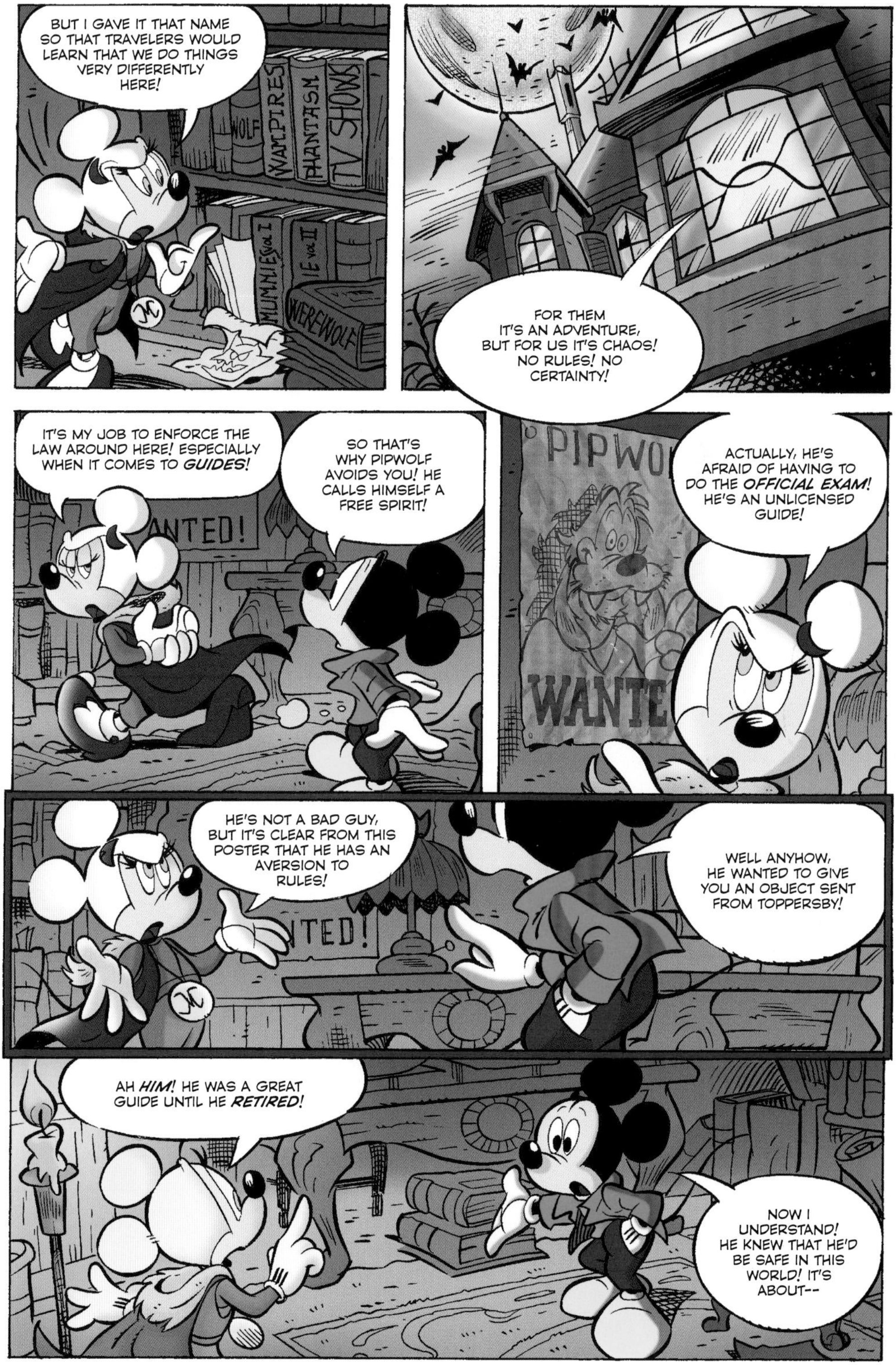
BUT I GAVE IT THAT NAME SO THAT TRAVELERS WOULD LEARN THAT WE DO THINGS VERY DIFFERENTLY HERE!
WOLF
VAMPIRES
PHANTASM
TV SHOWS
MUMMIES vol I
IE vol II
WEREWOLF
FOR THEM IT'S AN ADVENTURE, BUT FOR US IT'S CHAOS! NO RULES! NO CERTAINTY!
IT'S MY JOB TO ENFORCE THE LAW AROUND HERE! ESPECIALLY WHEN IT COMES TO GUIDES!
SO THAT'S WHY PIPWOLF AVOIDS YOU! HE CALLS HIMSELF A FREE SPIRIT!
ANTED!
PIPWO
WANTE
ACTUALLY, HE'S AFRAID OF HAVING TO DO THE OFFICIAL EXAM! HE'S AN UNLICENSED GUIDE!
HE'S NOT A BAD GUY, BUT IT'S CLEAR FROM THIS POSTER THAT HE HAS AN AVERSION TO RULES!
WELL ANYHOW, HE WANTED TO GIVE YOU AN OBJECT SENT FROM TOPPERSBY!
AH HIM! HE WAS A GREAT GUIDE UNTIL HE RETIRED!
NOW I UNDERSTAND! HE KNEW THAT HE'D BE SAFE IN THIS WORLD! IT'S ABOUT--

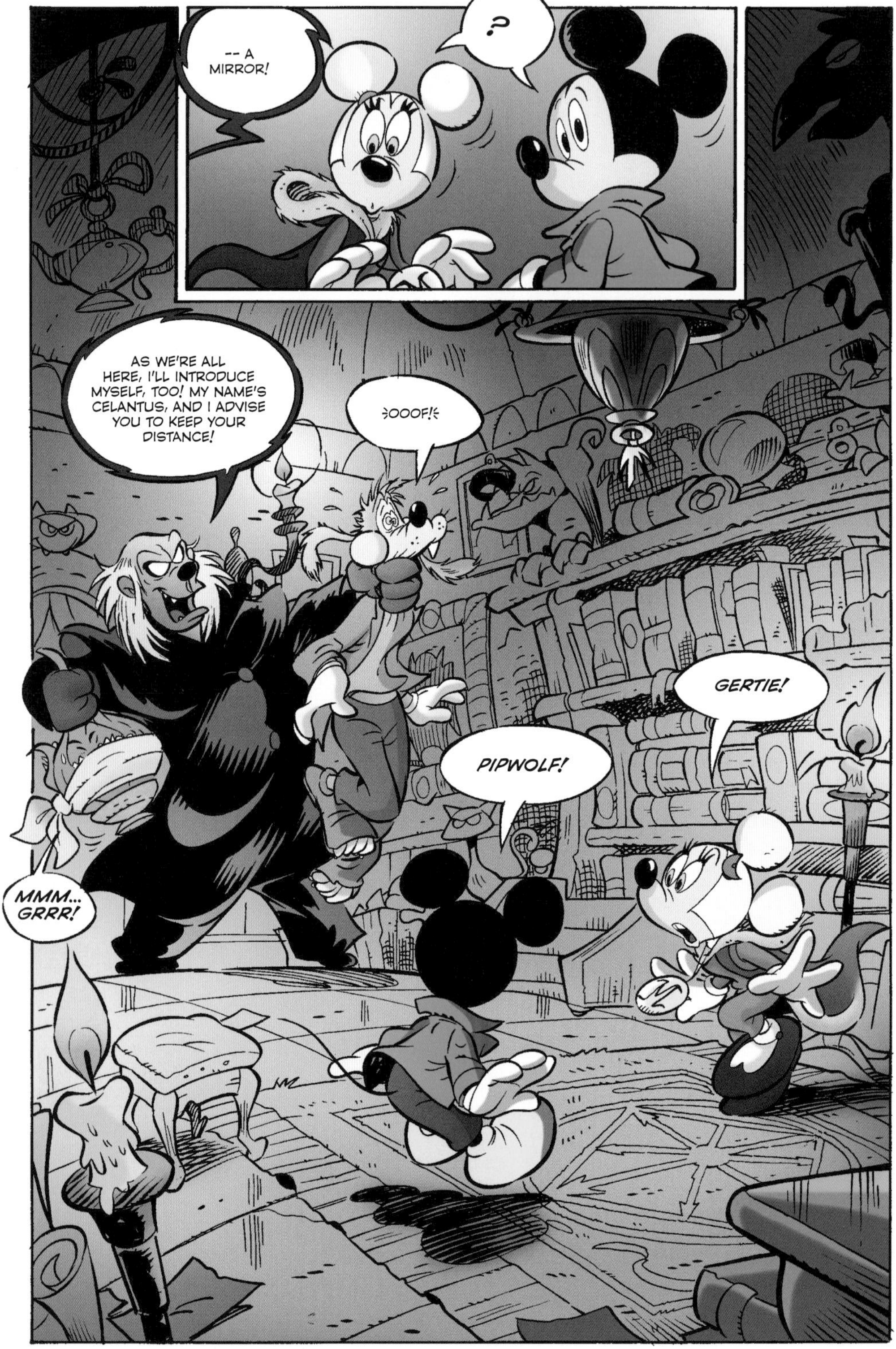
-- A MIRROR!
?
AS WE'RE ALL HERE, I'LL INTRODUCE MYSELF, TOO! MY NAME'S CELANTUS, AND I ADVISE YOU TO KEEP YOUR DISTANCE!
OOOF!
GERTIE!
PIPWOLF!
MMM... GRRR!

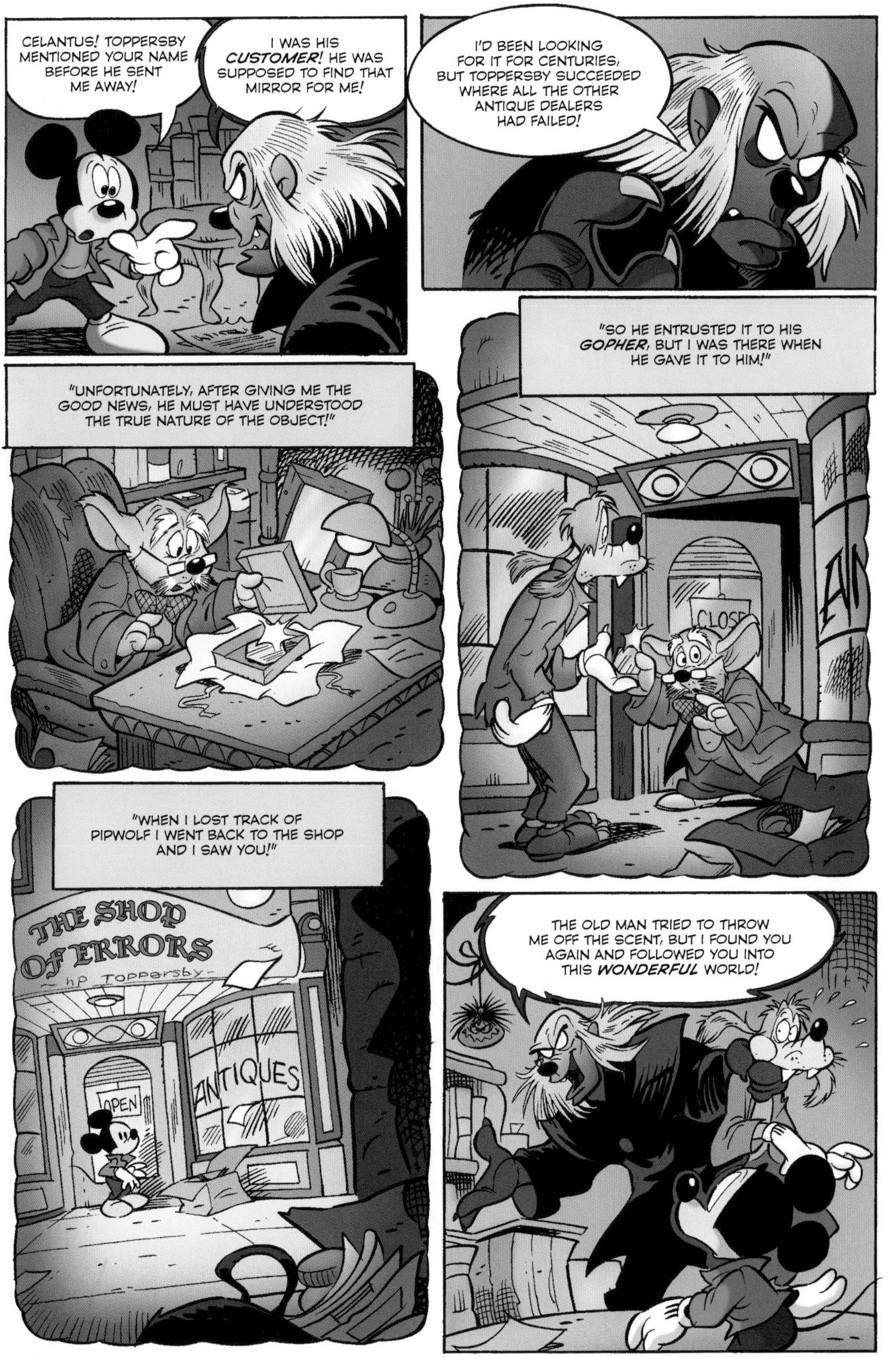
CELANTUS! TOPPERSBY MENTIONED YOUR NAME BEFORE HE SENT ME AWAY!
I WAS HIS CUSTOMER! HE WAS SUPPOSED TO FIND THAT MIRROR FOR ME!
I'D BEEN LOOKING FOR IT FOR CENTURIES, BUT TOPPERSBY SUCCEEDED WHERE ALL THE OTHER ANTIQUE DEALERS HAD FAILED!
"UNFORTUNATELY, AFTER GIVING ME THE GOOD NEWS, HE MUST HAVE UNDERSTOOD THE TRUE NATURE OF THE OBJECT!"
"SO HE ENTRUSTED IT TO HIS GOPHER, BUT I WAS THERE WHEN HE GAVE IT TO HIM!"
"WHEN I LOST TRACK OF PIPWOLF I WENT BACK TO THE SHOP AND I SAW YOU!"
THE SHOP OF ERRORS
~ hp Toppersby ~
OPEN
ANTIQUES
THE OLD MAN TRIED TO THROW ME OFF THE SCENT, BUT I FOUND YOU AGAIN AND FOLLOWED YOU INTO THIS WONDERFUL WORLD!

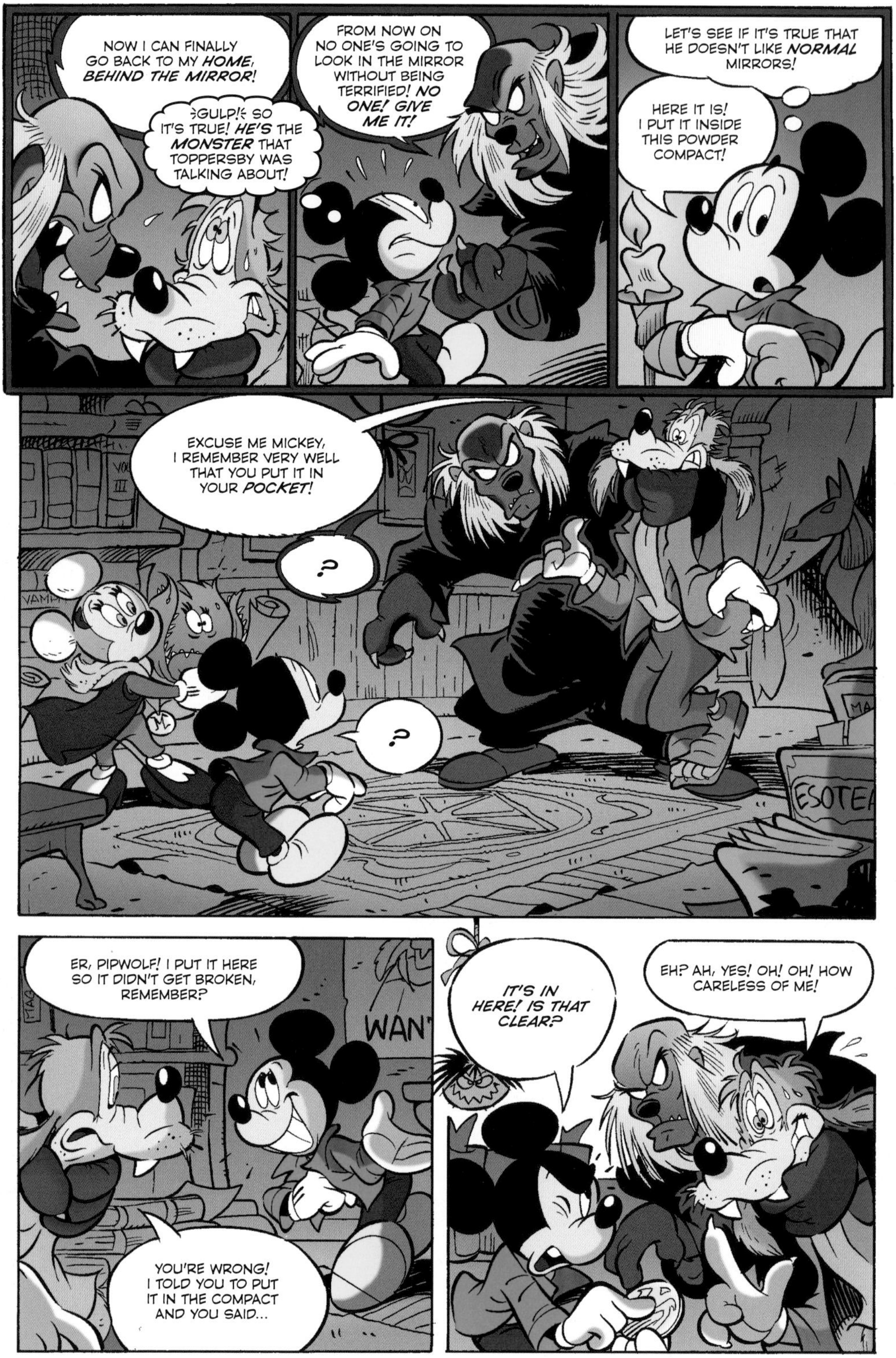
NOW I CAN FINALLY GO BACK TO MY HOME, BEHIND THE MIRROR!
GULP! SO IT'S TRUE! HE'S THE MONSTER THAT TOPPERSBY WAS TALKING ABOUT!
FROM NOW ON NO ONE'S GOING TO LOOK IN THE MIRROR WITHOUT BEING TERRIFIED! NO ONE! GIVE ME IT!
LET'S SEE IF IT'S TRUE THAT HE DOESN'T LIKE NORMAL MIRRORS!
HERE IT IS! I PUT IT INSIDE THIS POWDER COMPACT!
EXCUSE ME MICKEY, I REMEMBER VERY WELL THAT YOU PUT IT IN YOUR POCKET!
?
?
ESOTER
ER, PIPWOLF! I PUT IT HERE SO IT DIDN'T GET BROKEN, REMEMBER?
WAN
YOU'RE WRONG! I TOLD YOU TO PUT IT IN THE COMPACT AND YOU SAID...
IT'S IN HERE! IS THAT CLEAR?
EH? AH, YES! OH! OH! HOW CARELESS OF ME!

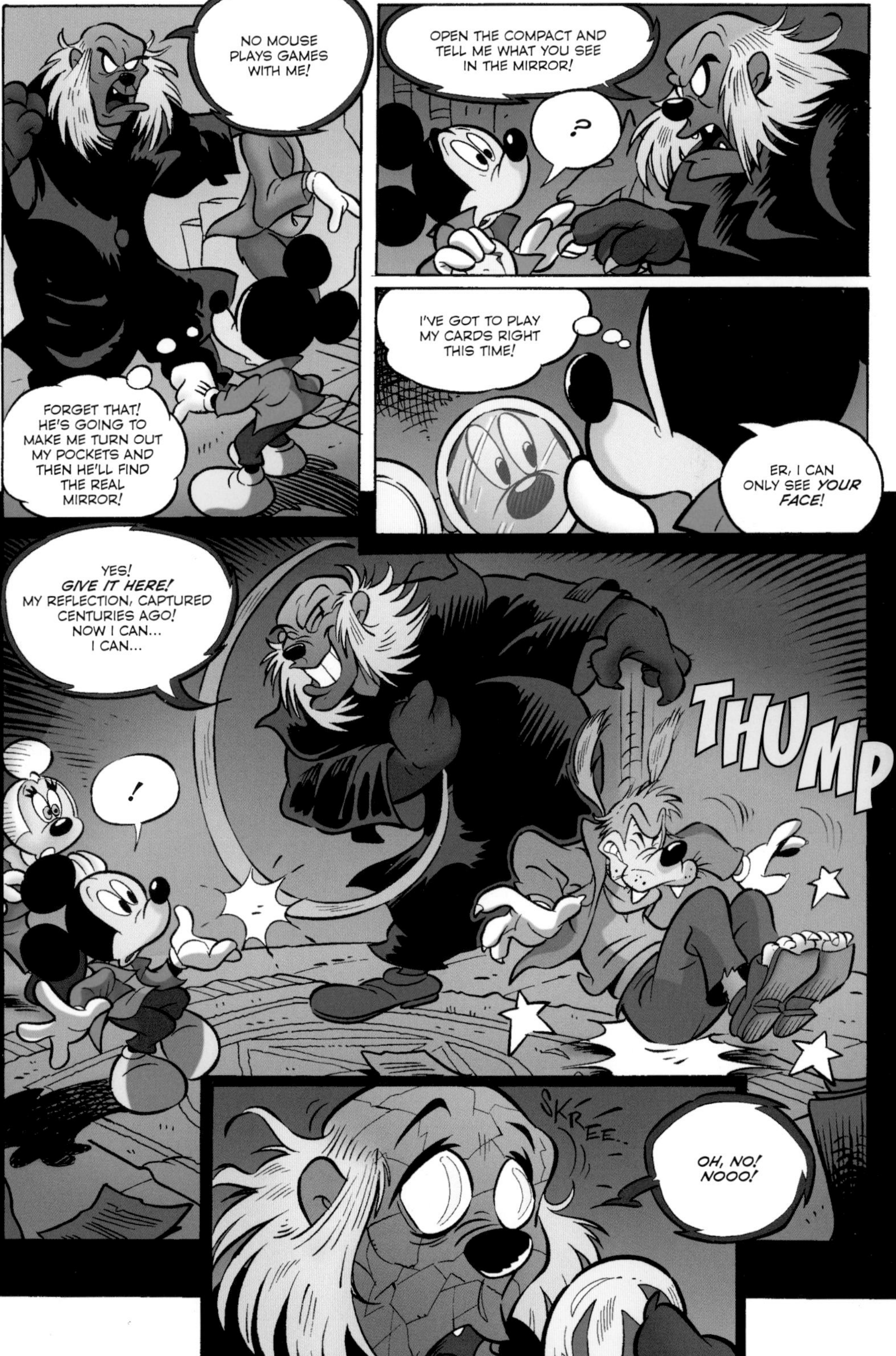
NO MOUSE PLAYS GAMES WITH ME!
FORGET THAT! HE'S GOING TO MAKE ME TURN OUT MY POCKETS AND THEN HE'LL FIND THE REAL MIRROR!
OPEN THE COMPACT AND TELL ME WHAT YOU SEE IN THE MIRROR!
?
I'VE GOT TO PLAY MY CARDS RIGHT THIS TIME!
ER, I CAN ONLY SEE YOUR FACE!
YES! GIVE IT HERE! MY REFLECTION, CAPTURED CENTURIES AGO! NOW I CAN... I CAN...
!
THUMP
SKREEE...
OH, NO! NOOO!

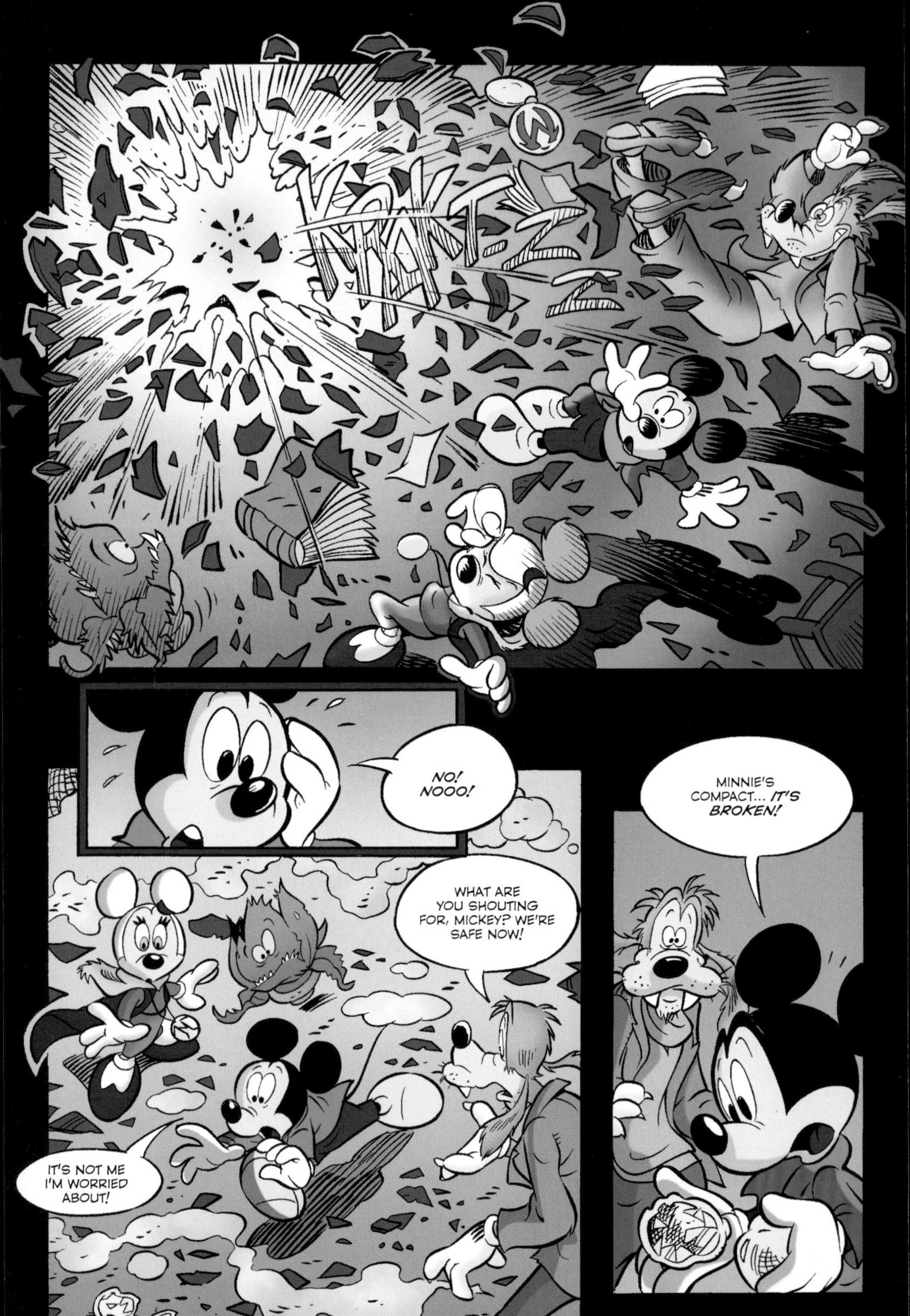
NO! NOOO!
WHAT ARE YOU SHOUTING FOR, MICKEY? WE'RE SAFE NOW!
IT'S NOT ME I'M WORRIED ABOUT!
MINNIE'S COMPACT... IT'S BROKEN!

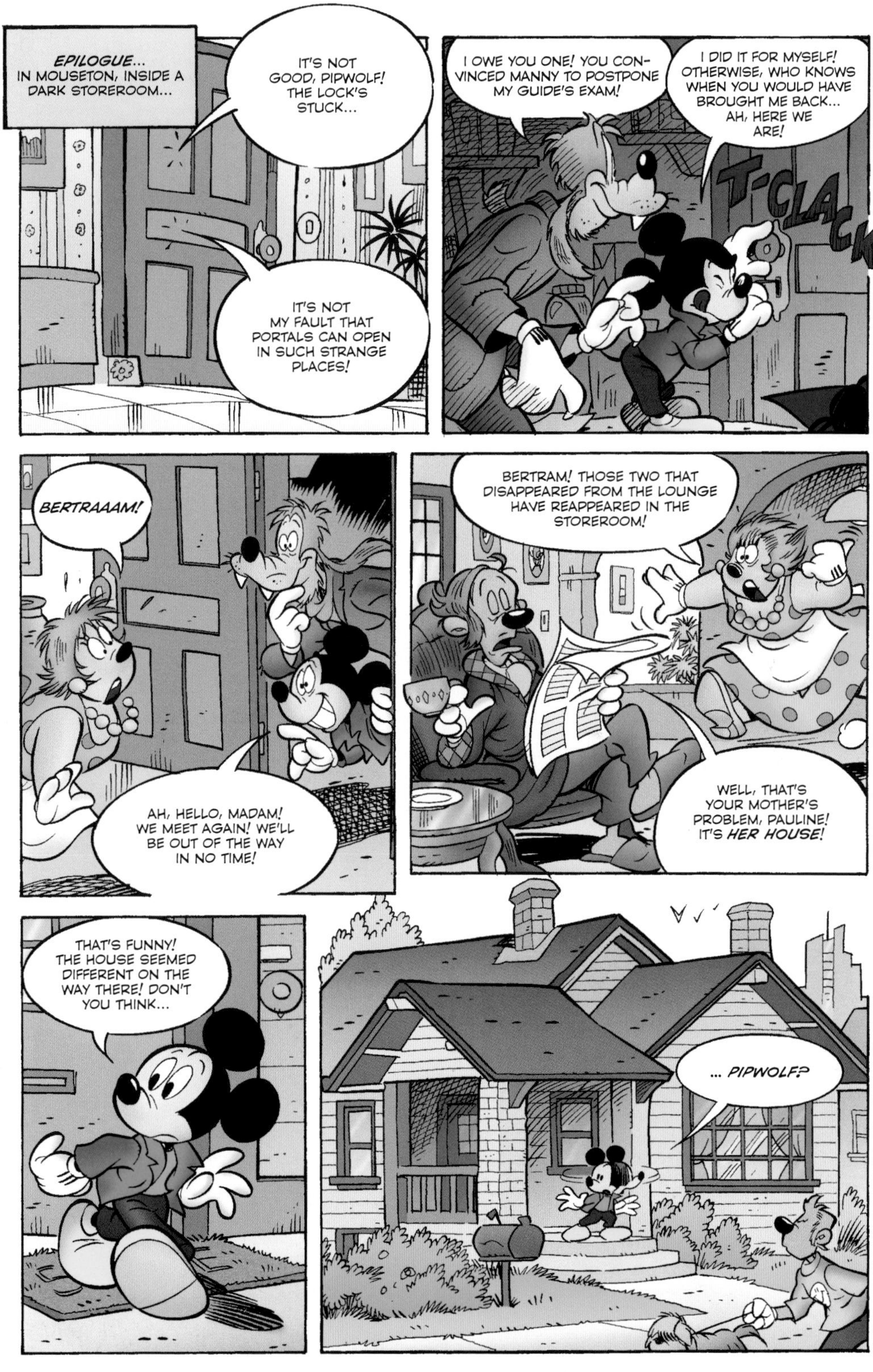
EPILOGUE... IN MOUSETON, INSIDE A DARK STOREROOM...
IT'S NOT GOOD, PIPWOLF! THE LOCK'S STUCK...
IT'S NOT MY FAULT THAT PORTALS CAN OPEN IN SUCH STRANGE PLACES!
I OWE YOU ONE! YOU CONVINCED MANNY TO POSTPONE MY GUIDE'S EXAM!
I DID IT FOR MYSELF! OTHERWISE, WHO KNOWS WHEN YOU WOULD HAVE BROUGHT ME BACK... AH, HERE WE ARE!
T-CLACK
BERTRAAAM!
AH, HELLO, MADAM! WE MEET AGAIN! WE'LL BE OUT OF THE WAY IN NO TIME!
BERTRAM! THOSE TWO THAT DISAPPEARED FROM THE LOUNGE HAVE REAPPEARED IN THE STOREROOM!
WELL, THAT'S YOUR MOTHER'S PROBLEM, PAULINE! IT'S HER HOUSE!
THAT'S FUNNY! THE HOUSE SEEMED DIFFERENT ON THE WAY THERE! DON'T YOU THINK...
... PIPWOLF?

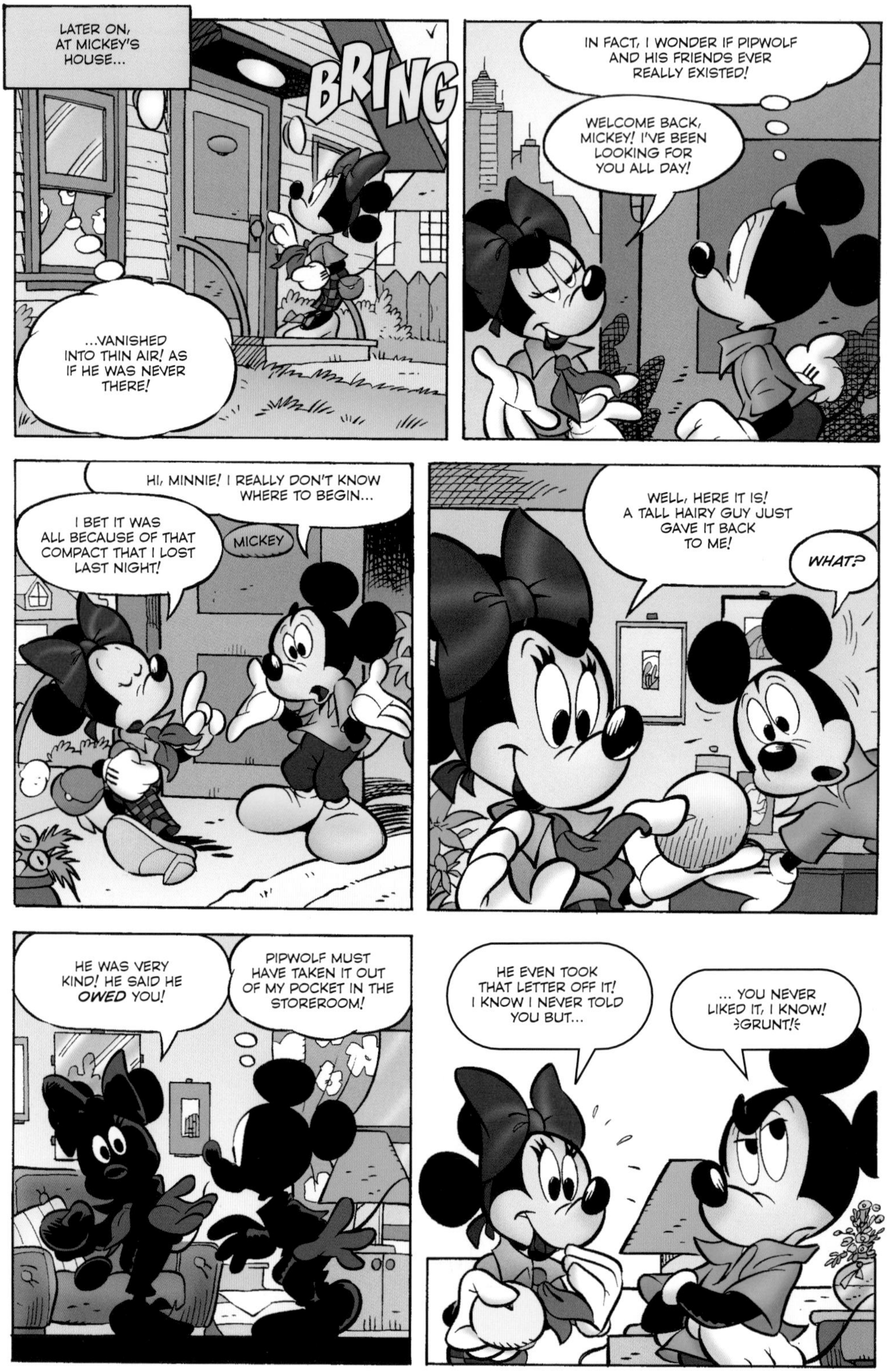
LATER ON, AT MICKEY'S HOUSE...
BRING
...VANISHED INTO THIN AIR! AS IF HE WAS NEVER THERE!
IN FACT, I WONDER IF PIPWOLF AND HIS FRIENDS EVER REALLY EXISTED!
WELCOME BACK, MICKEY! I'VE BEEN LOOKING FOR YOU ALL DAY!
HI, MINNIE! I REALLY DON'T KNOW WHERE TO BEGIN...
I BET IT WAS ALL BECAUSE OF THAT COMPACT THAT I LOST LAST NIGHT!
MICKEY
WELL, HERE IT IS! A TALL HAIRY GUY JUST GAVE IT BACK TO ME!
WHAT?
HE WAS VERY KIND! HE SAID HE *OWED* YOU!
PIPWOLF MUST HAVE TAKEN IT OUT OF MY POCKET IN THE STOREROOM!
HE EVEN TOOK THAT LETTER OFF IT! I KNOW I NEVER TOLD YOU BUT...
... YOU NEVER LIKED IT, I KNOW! GRUNT!

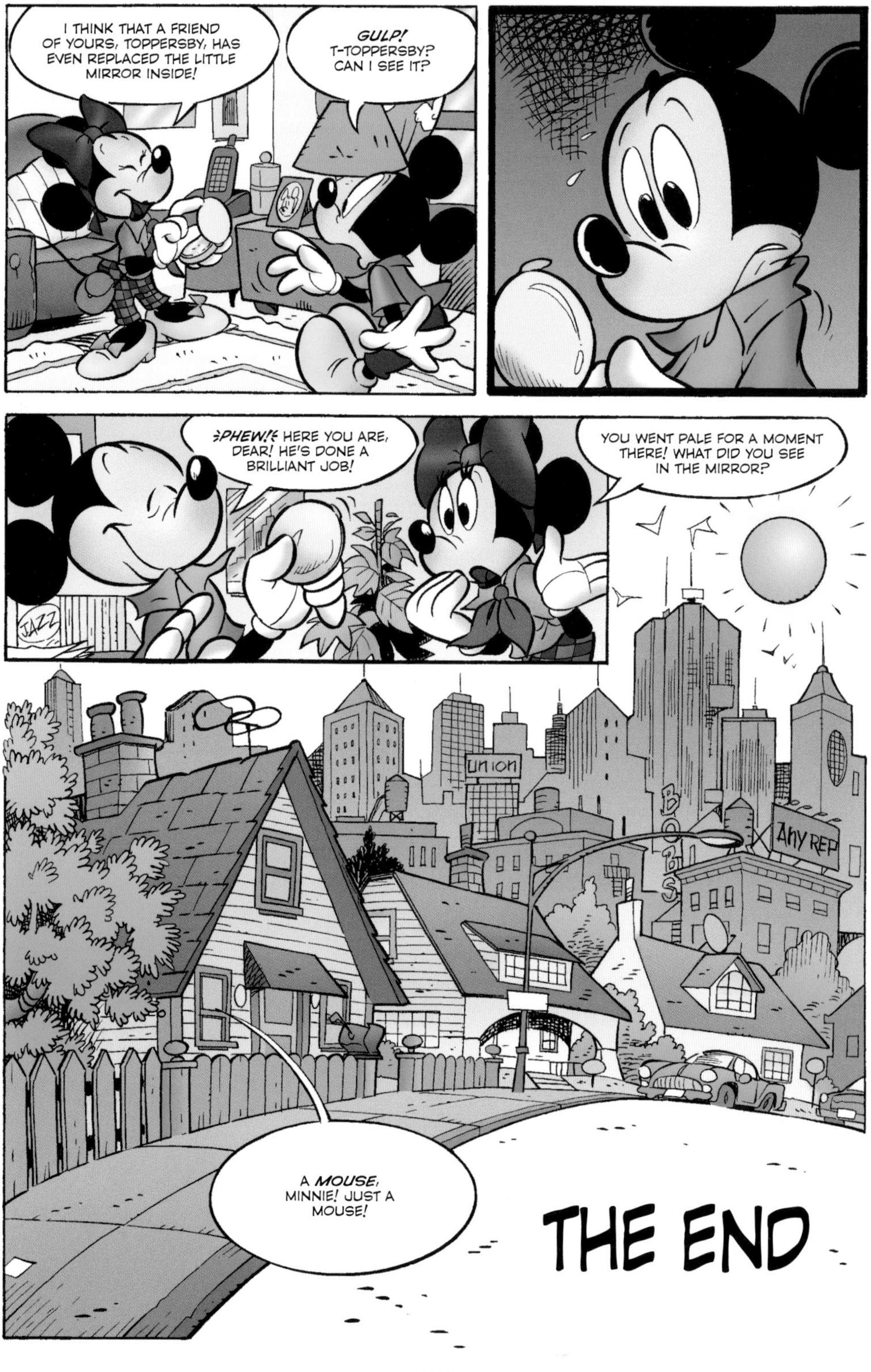
I THINK THAT A FRIEND OF YOURS, TOPPERSBY, HAS EVEN REPLACED THE LITTLE MIRROR INSIDE!
GULP! T-TOPPERSBY? CAN I SEE IT?
PHEW! HERE YOU ARE, DEAR! HE'S DONE A BRILLIANT JOB!
YOU WENT PALE FOR A MOMENT THERE! WHAT DID YOU SEE IN THE MIRROR?
JAZZ
UNION
BOBS
ANY REP
A MOUSE, MINNIE! JUST A MOUSE!
THE END

# WATCH OUT FOR PAPERCUTZ™

Welcome to the spooky second DISNEY GRAPHIC NOVELS graphic novel—that's not a typo, the secret real name of this series is DISNEY GRAPHIC NOVELS, but for various crazy reasons we're not actually calling it that on the cover. Instead it seems easier to simply call this the very first DISNEY X-MICKEY graphic novel.

Why X-MICKEY? Good question! Let's just say, when this story first appeared in Italy, on April 30, 1998, there was a TV series that explored the paranormal that was very popular, and there's been a long history of using the letter X to denote the unknown and the mysterious, thus X-MICKEY was born. X-MICKEY is a series that features the one and only Mickey Mouse exploring all sorts of strange and spooky stuff. So, how exciting is that?

But even more meaningful to me—oops, I forgot to introduce myself. I'm Jim Salicrup, the Editor-in-Chief of Papercutz (and a one-time guest on the Mickey Mouse Club TV show), the comics company dedicated to publishing great graphic novels for all ages. So, as I was saying, what's even more meaningful to me is that Papercutz is at long last publishing an honest-to-gawrsh series starring Mickey Mouse. Just as Superman is the very first, and perhaps most important, comicbook superhero ever, Mickey Mouse is one of the earliest, and one of the most important cartoon characters ever. As Walt Disney himself would often remind his co-workers, as the Disney company kept growing more and more successful, "I hope we never lose sight of one thing, that it was all started by a mouse."

And it's great to see that Mickey Mouse is roaring back into American comics, in all sorts of forms. In fact, several great comics publishers are all presenting great examples of Mickey's colorful comics career. WALT DISNEY'S MICKEY MOUSE, a handsome deluxe hardcover series, that collects Floyd Gottfredson Mickey Mouse comics strips, which is published by our friends at Fantagraphics, while IDW has recently re-launched the long-running WALT DISNEY'S MICKEY MOUSE comicbook, featuring exciting Mickey Mouse adventures created by writers and artists from around the world. Not only will Papercutz be publishing X-MICKEY, we'll be featuring the fun adventures of Minnie Mouse and Daisy Duck in a series of graphic novels entitled DISNEY MINNIE AND DAISY! Plus we'll also be presenting another graphic novel series called DISNEY GREAT PARODIES that will recast the greatest works of literature (or shout we say liteRATure?) with classic Disney characters. We can't wait to publish Mickey's Inferno—the one that started the GREAT PARODIES series.

We hope you enjoyed this premiere installment of X-MICKEY, written by Bruno Enna and drawn by Alessandro Perina, and enjoy all the Disney Comics now available at bookstores and comic shops. Not to mention the following bonus pages from DISNEY FAIRIES #18 "Tinker Bell and her Magical Friends."

And remember... The Goof is out there!

Thanks, Jim

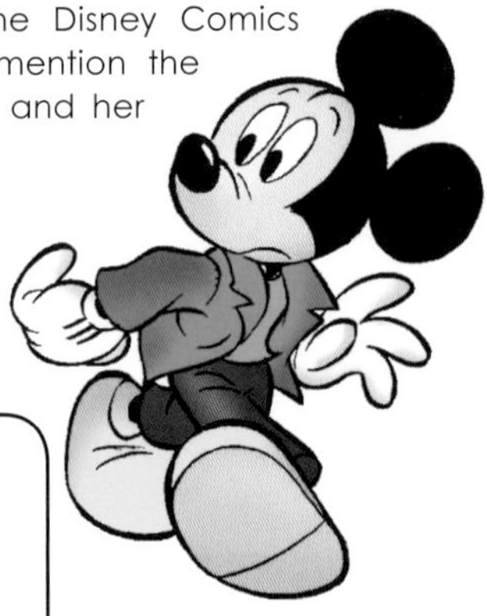

## STAY IN TOUCH!

| | |
|---|---|
| EMAIL: | salicrup@papercutz.com |
| WEB: | papercutz.com |
| TWITTER: | @papercutzgn |
| FACEBOOK: | PAPERCUTZGRAPHICNOVELS |
| FAN MAIL: | Papercutz, 160 Broadway, Suite 700, East Wing, New York, NY 10038 |

Special Preview of DISNEY FAIRIES #18 “Tinker Bell and her Magical Friends”...

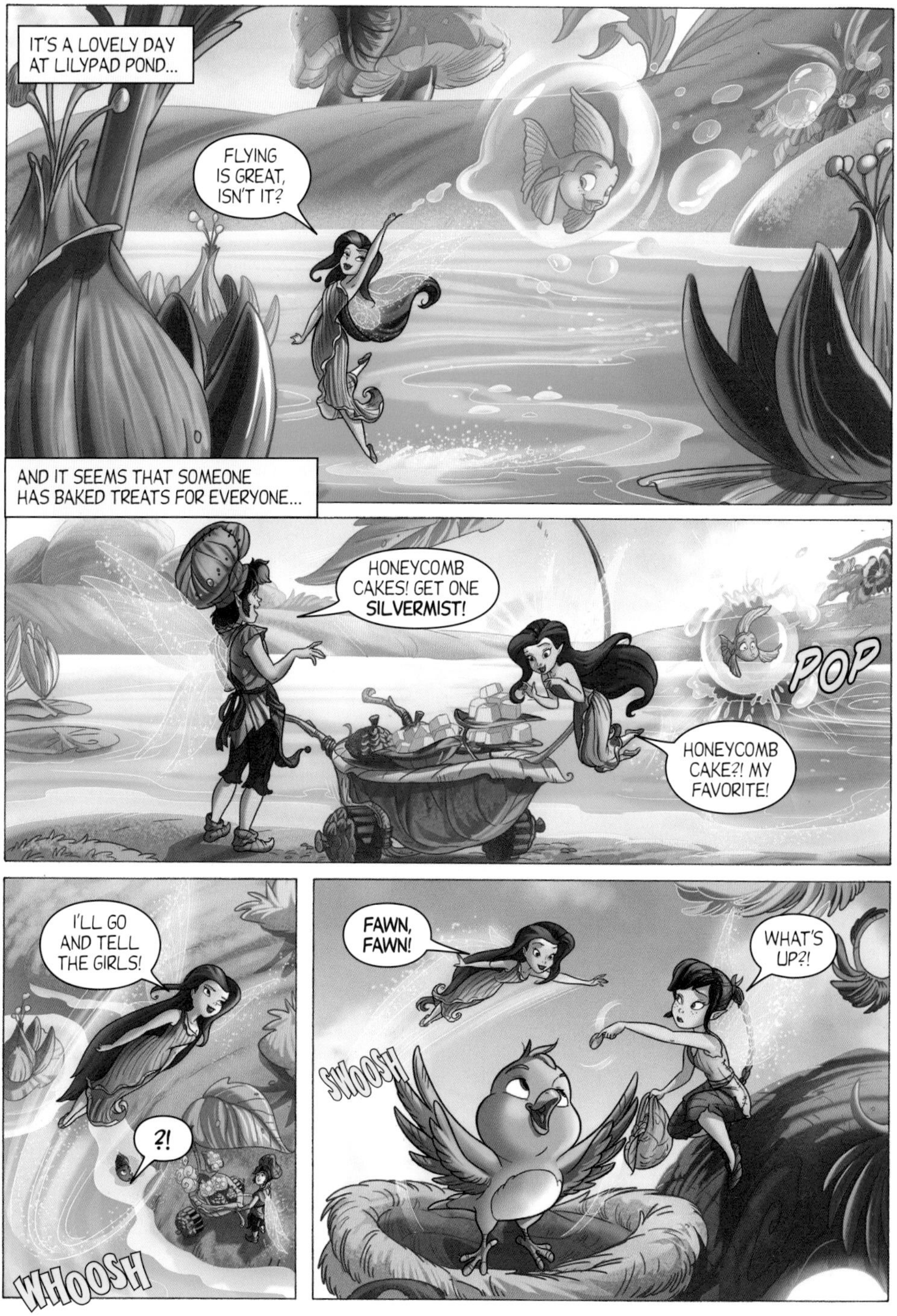
IT'S A LOVELY DAY AT LILYPAD POND...
FLYING IS GREAT, ISN'T IT?
AND IT SEEMS THAT SOMEONE HAS BAKED TREATS FOR EVERYONE...
HONEYCOMB CAKES! GET ONE SILVERMIST!
POP
HONEYCOMB CAKE?! MY FAVORITE!
I'LL GO AND TELL THE GIRLS!
?!
WHOOSH
FAWN, FAWN!
WHAT'S UP?!
SWOOSH

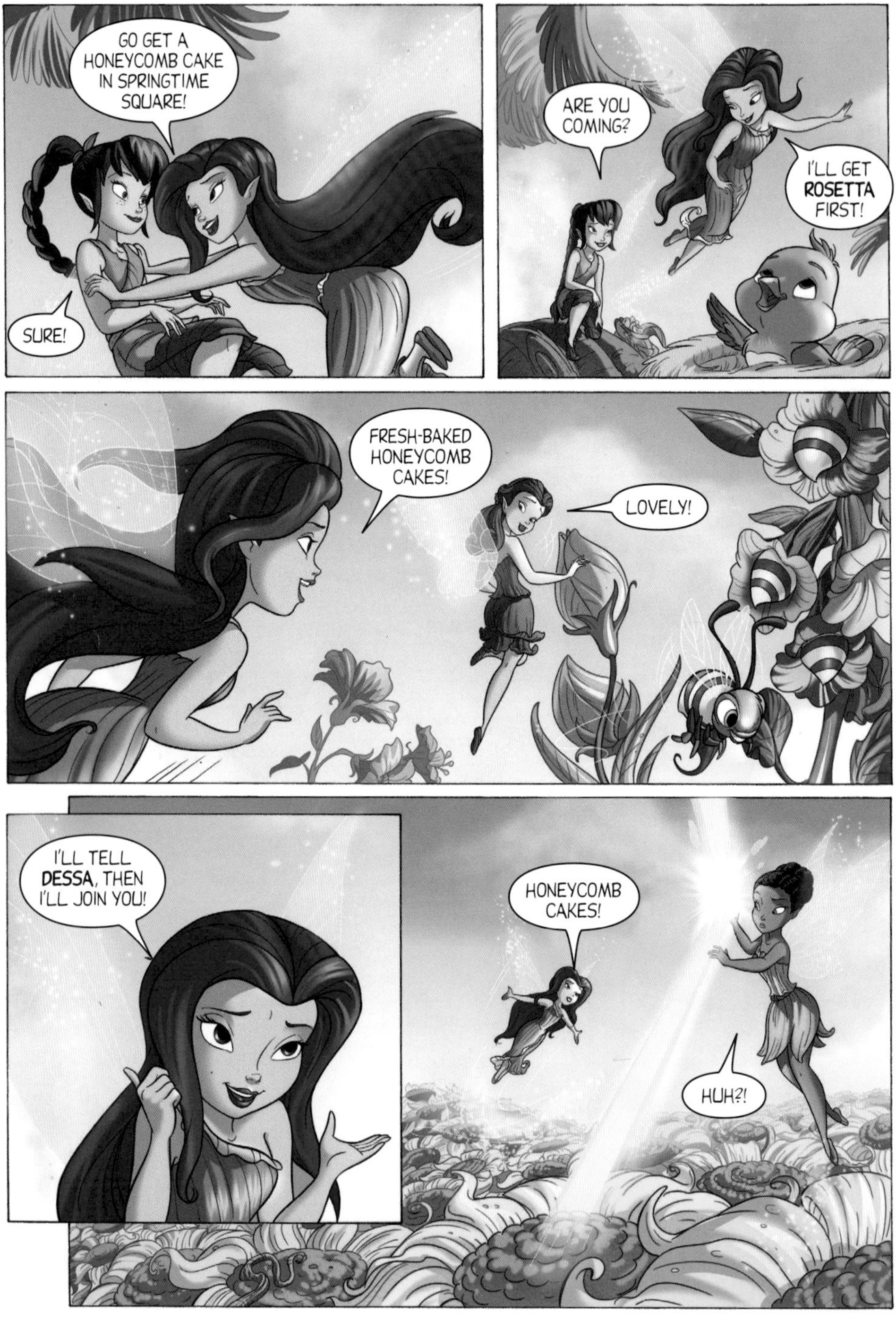
GO GET A HONEYCOMB CAKE IN SPRINGTIME SQUARE!
SURE!
ARE YOU COMING?
I'LL GET ROSETTA FIRST!
FRESH-BAKED HONEYCOMB CAKES!
LOVELY!
I'LL TELL DESSA, THEN I'LL JOIN YOU!
HONEYCOMB CAKES!
HUH?!

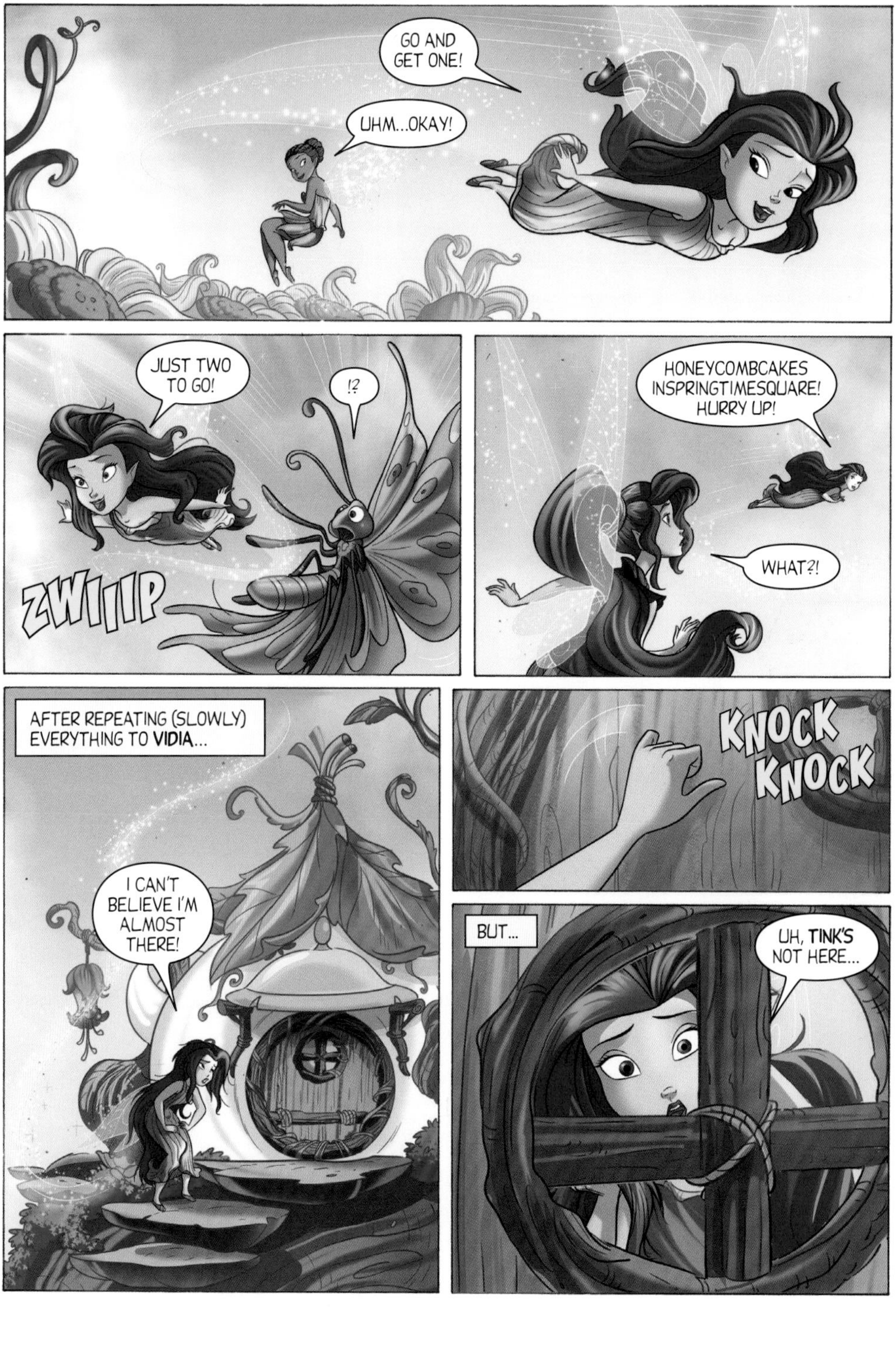
GO AND GET ONE!
UHM...OKAY!
JUST TWO TO GO!
!?
ZWIIIP
HONEYCOMBCAKES INSPRINGTIMESQUARE! HURRY UP!
WHAT?!
AFTER REPEATING (SLOWLY) EVERYTHING TO VIDIA...
I CAN'T BELIEVE I'M ALMOST THERE!
KNOCK KNOCK
BUT...
UH, TINK'S NOT HERE...

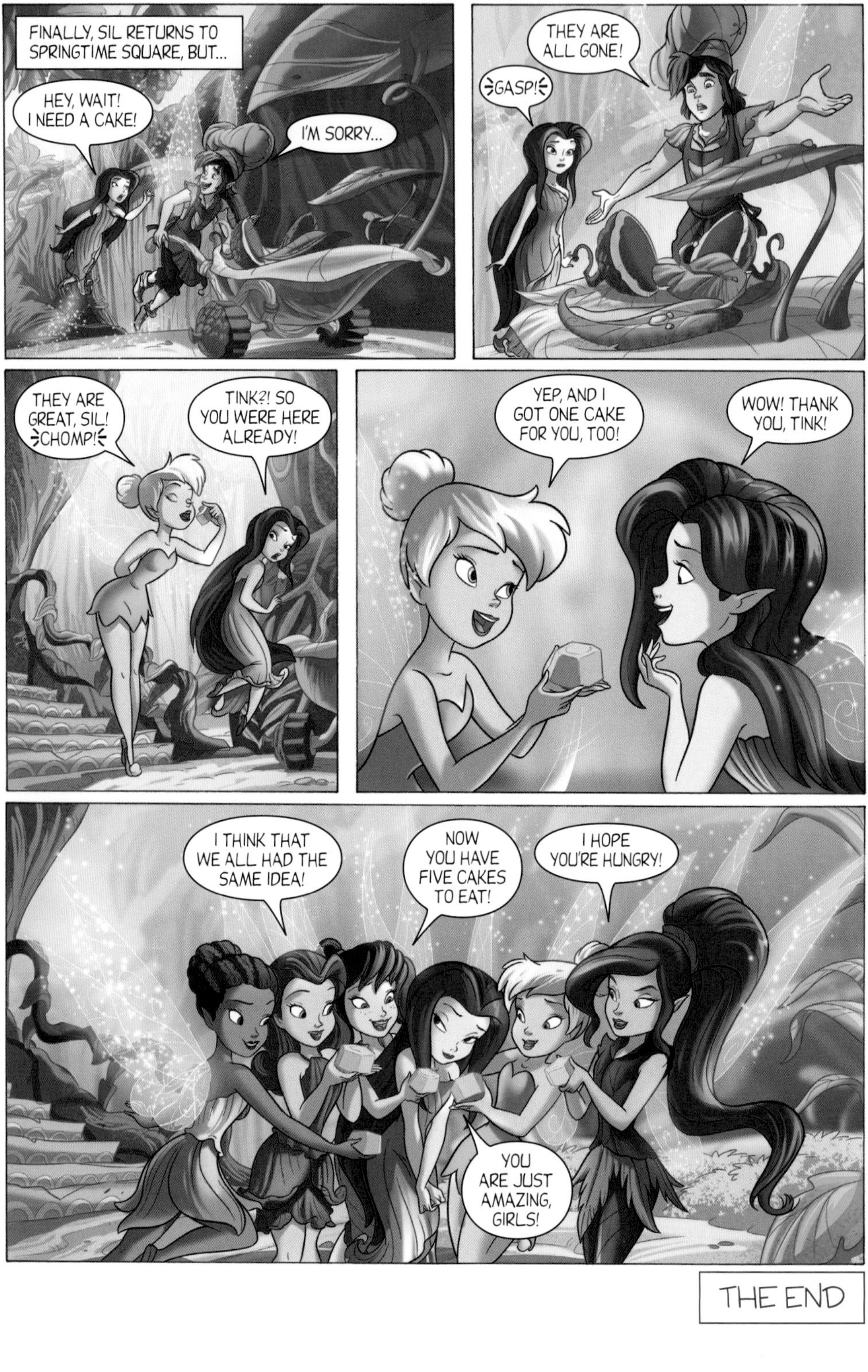
FINALLY, SIL RETURNS TO SPRINGTIME SQUARE, BUT...
HEY, WAIT! I NEED A CAKE!
I'M SORRY...
THEY ARE ALL GONE!
GASP!
THEY ARE GREAT, SIL! CHOMP!
TINK?! SO YOU WERE HERE ALREADY!
YEP, AND I GOT ONE CAKE FOR YOU, TOO!
WOW! THANK YOU, TINK!
I THINK THAT WE ALL HAD THE SAME IDEA!
NOW YOU HAVE FIVE CAKES TO EAT!
I HOPE YOU'RE HUNGRY!
YOU ARE JUST AMAZING, GIRLS!
THE END

# Beautiful Ribbons

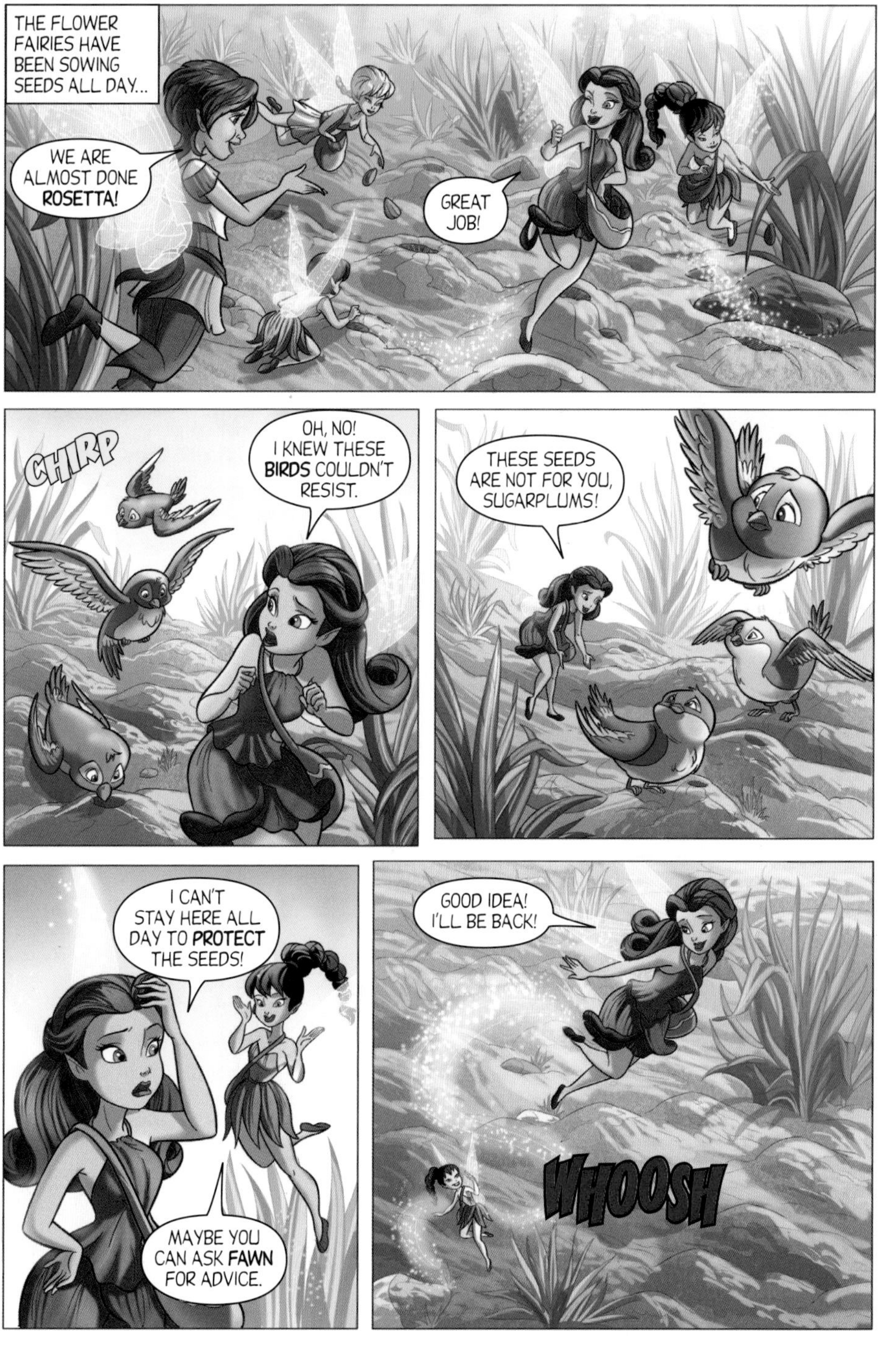

THE FLOWER FAIRIES HAVE BEEN SOWING SEEDS ALL DAY...
WE ARE ALMOST DONE **ROSETTA!**
GREAT JOB!
CHIRP
OH, NO! I KNEW THESE **BIRDS** COULDN'T RESIST.
THESE SEEDS ARE NOT FOR YOU, SUGARPLUMS!
I CAN'T STAY HERE ALL DAY TO **PROTECT** THE SEEDS!
MAYBE YOU CAN ASK **FAWN** FOR ADVICE.
GOOD IDEA! I'LL BE BACK!
WHOOSH

RO REACHES FAWN AND TELLS HER ABOUT THE PROBLEM...

YOU CAN BUILD A **PUPPET** IN THE MIDDLE OF THE FIELD.

A PUPPET?

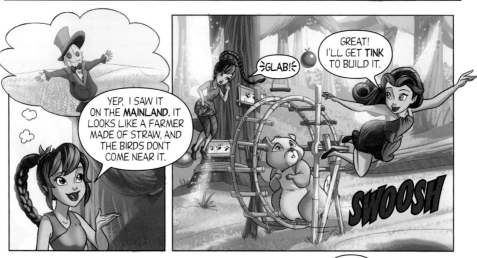

YEP, I SAW IT ON THE **MAINLAND.** IT LOOKS LIKE A FARMER MADE OF STRAW, AND THE BIRDS DON'T COME NEAR IT.

⇥GLAB!⇤

GREAT! I'LL GET **TINK** TO BUILD IT.

SWOOSH

NO SOONER SAID THAN DONE...

WHOA! YOU'RE AMAZING, TINK!

THANKS, WE JUST NEED TO ADD THE **FINISHING TOUCHES** NOW.

WHAT IS IT?

LET'S GO TO **THE WORKSHOP,** AND YOU'LL FIND OUT.

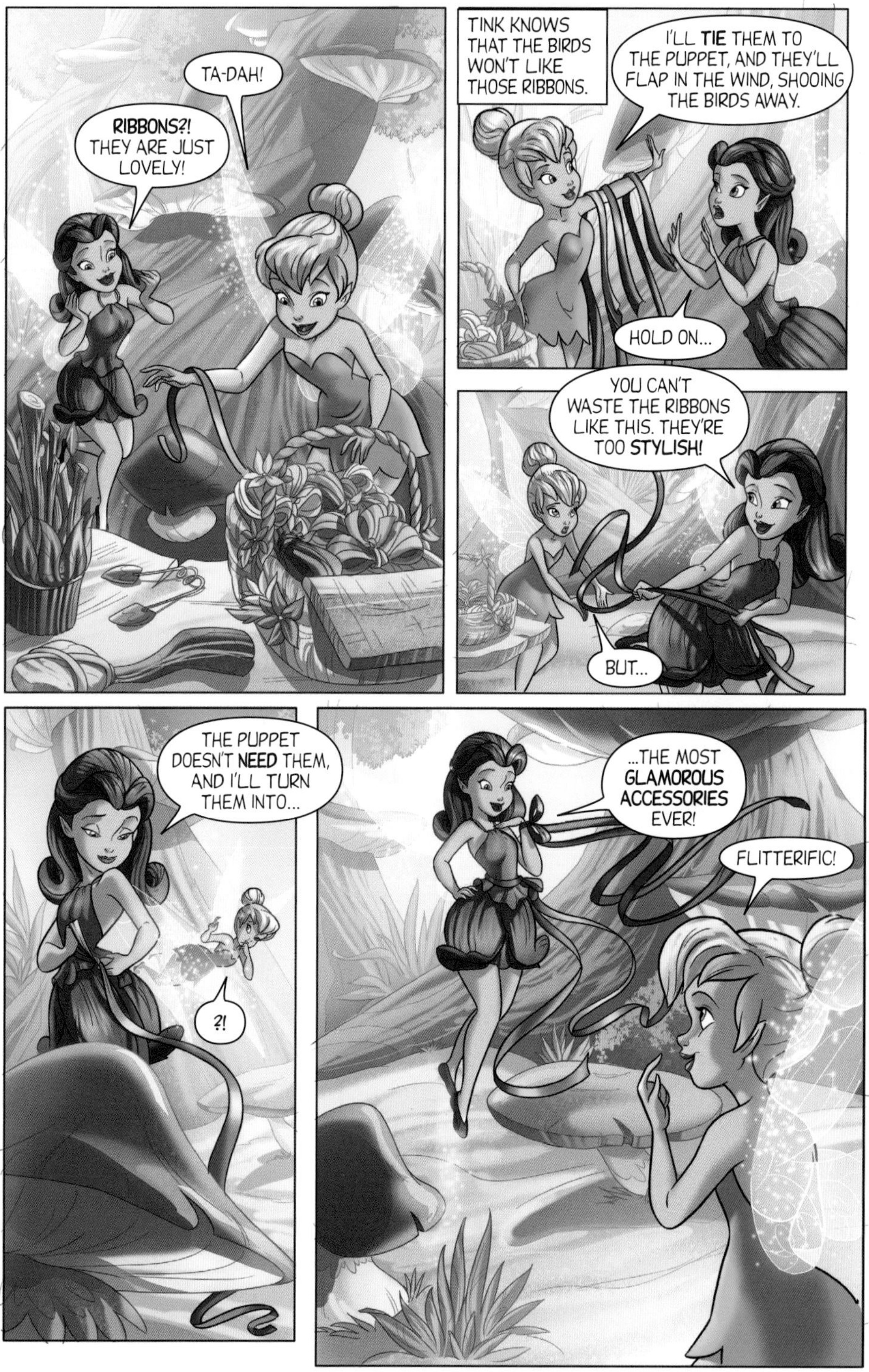
TA-DAH!
RIBBONS?! THEY ARE JUST LOVELY!
TINK KNOWS THAT THE BIRDS WON'T LIKE THOSE RIBBONS.
I'LL TIE THEM TO THE PUPPET, AND THEY'LL FLAP IN THE WIND, SHOOING THE BIRDS AWAY.
HOLD ON...
YOU CAN'T WASTE THE RIBBONS LIKE THIS. THEY'RE TOO STYLISH!
BUT...
THE PUPPET DOESN'T NEED THEM, AND I'LL TURN THEM INTO...
?!
...THE MOST GLAMOROUS ACCESSORIES EVER!
FLITTERIFIC!

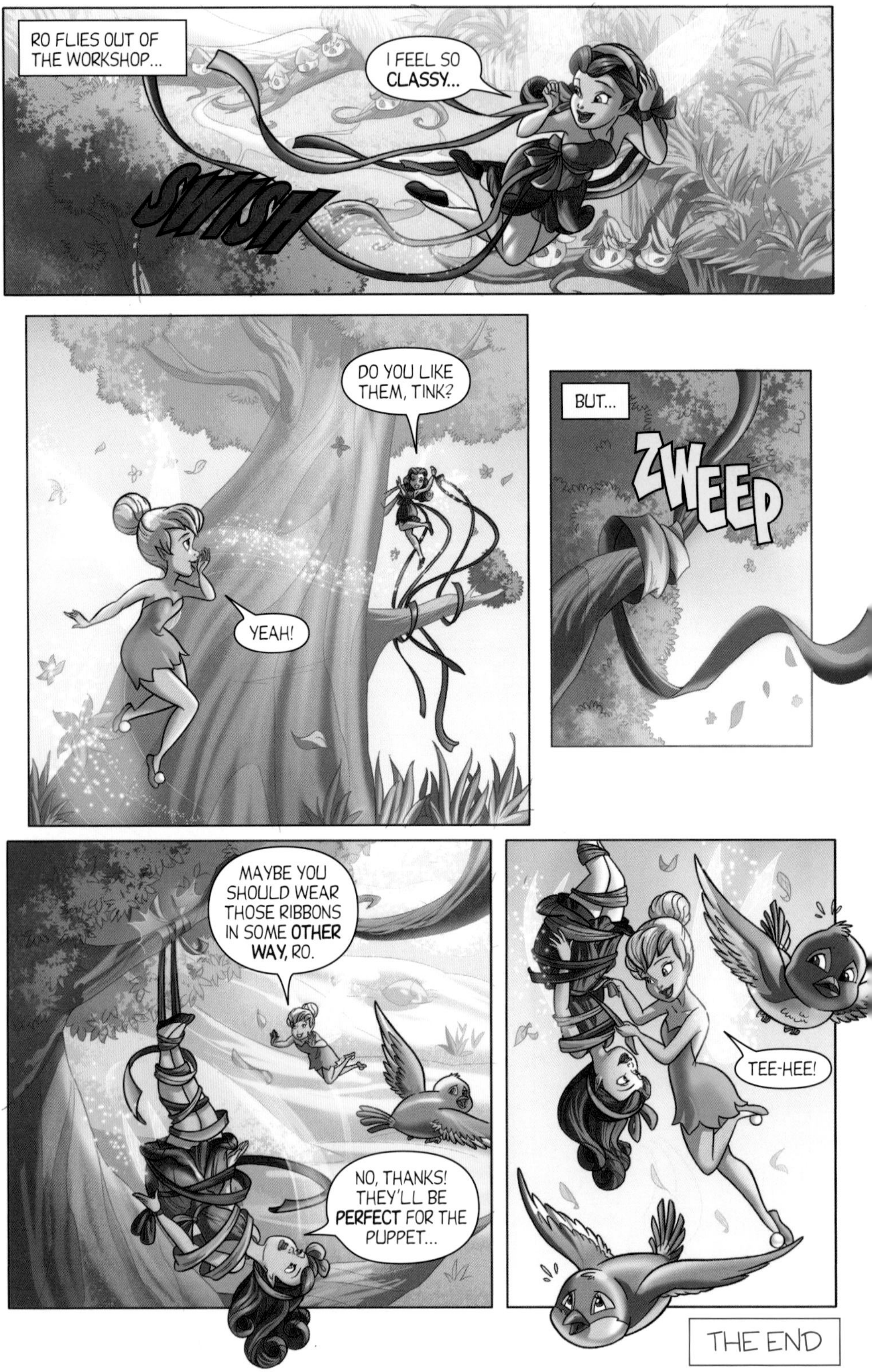
RO FLIES OUT OF THE WORKSHOP...
I FEEL SO CLASSY...
SWISH
DO YOU LIKE THEM, TINK?
YEAH!
BUT...
ZWEEP
MAYBE YOU SHOULD WEAR THOSE RIBBONS IN SOME OTHER WAY, RO.
NO, THANKS! THEY'LL BE PERFECT FOR THE PUPPET...
TEE-HEE!
THE END

# Hop, Hop!

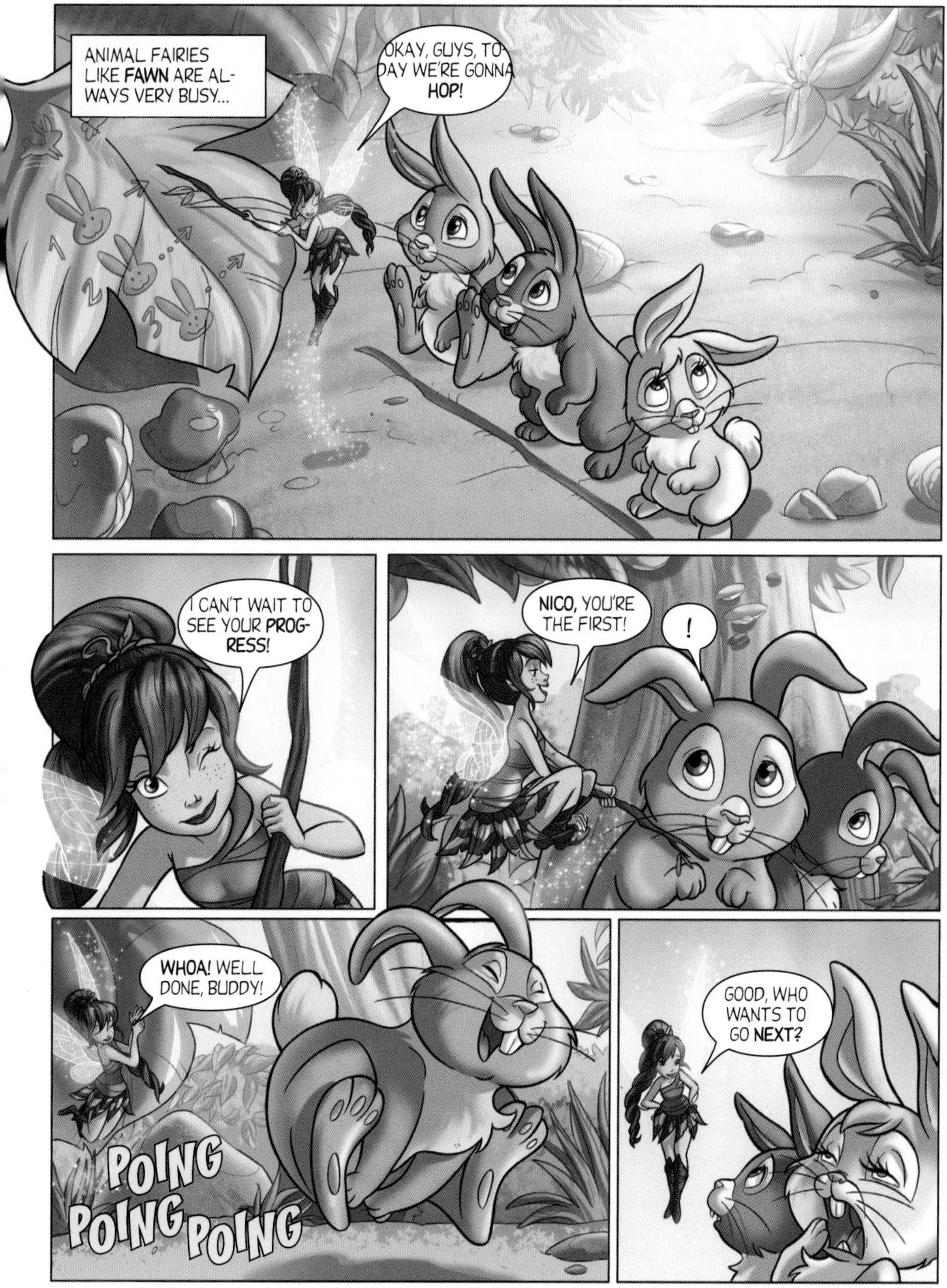

ANIMAL FAIRIES LIKE **FAWN** ARE AL-WAYS VERY BUSY...
OKAY, GUYS, TO-DAY WE'RE GONNA **HOP!**
I CAN'T WAIT TO SEE YOUR **PROG-RESS!**
**NICO**, YOU'RE THE FIRST!
!
**WHOA!** WELL DONE, BUDDY!
POING POING POING
GOOD, WHO WANTS TO GO **NEXT?**

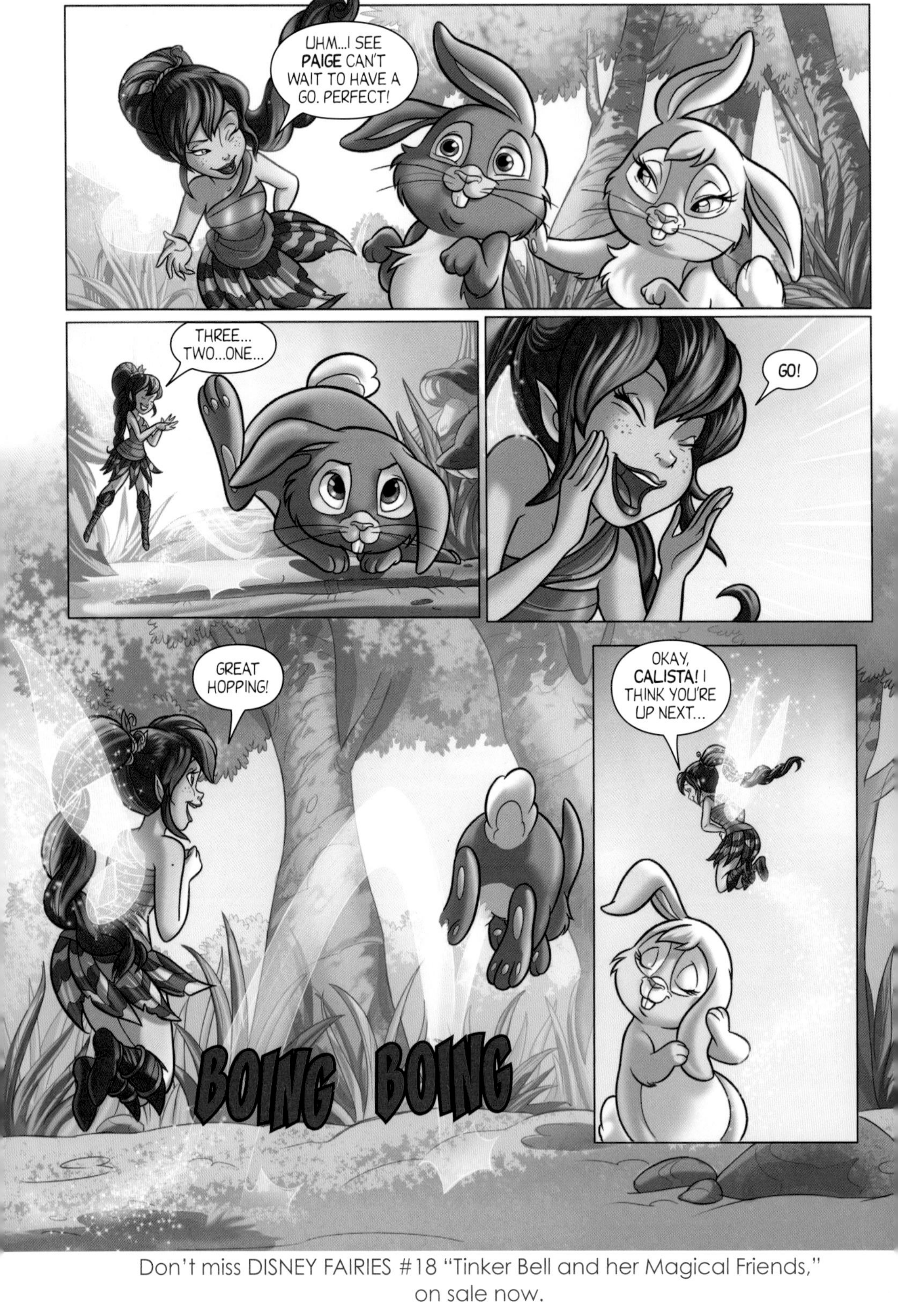
UHM...I SEE PAIGE CAN'T WAIT TO HAVE A GO. PERFECT!
THREE... TWO...ONE...
GO!
GREAT HOPPING!
BOING BOING
OKAY, CALISTA! I THINK YOU'RE UP NEXT...

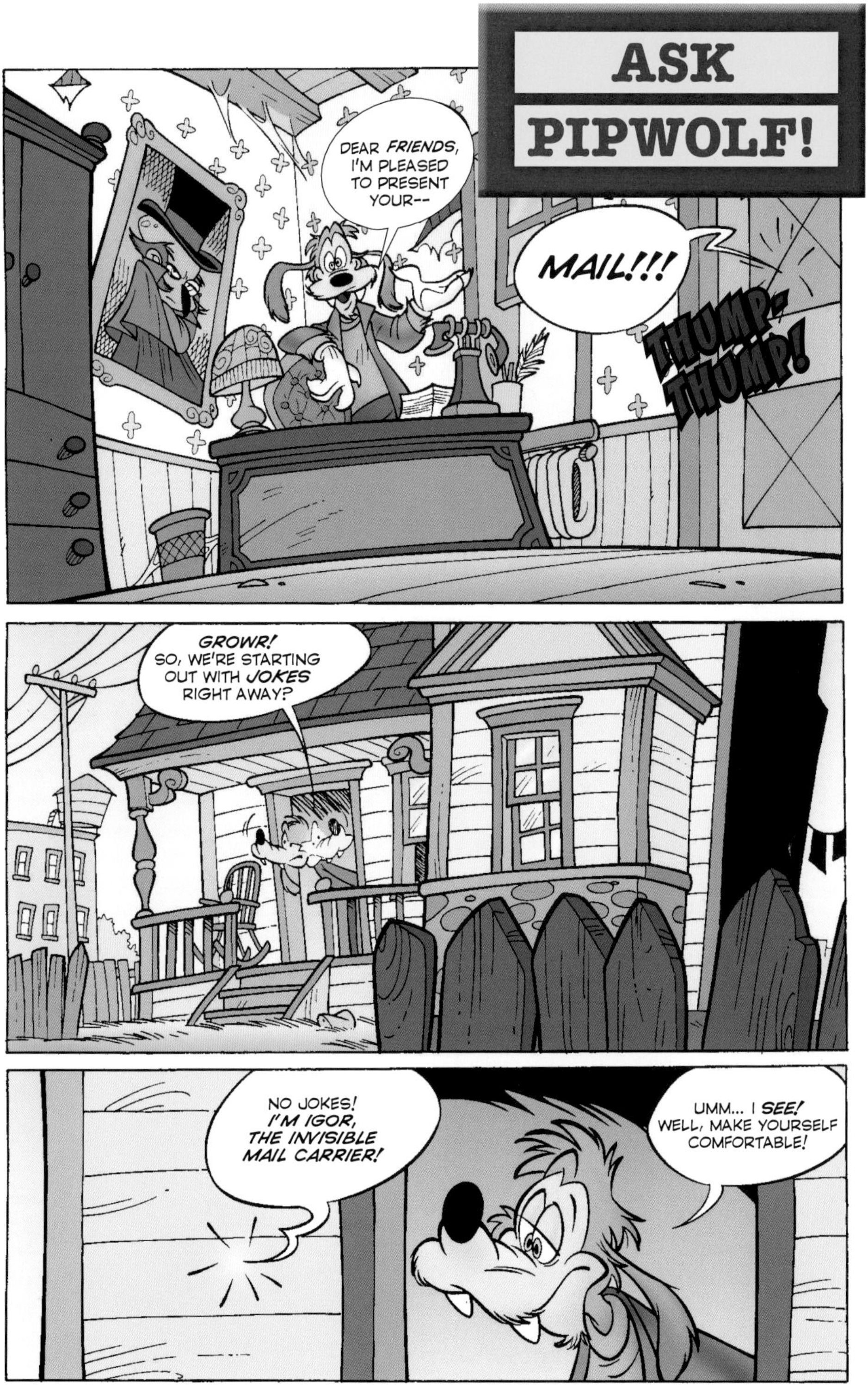
ASK PIPWOLF!
DEAR FRIENDS, I'M PLEASED TO PRESENT YOUR--
MAIL!!!
THUMP-THUMP!
GROWR! SO, WE'RE STARTING OUT WITH JOKES RIGHT AWAY?
NO JOKES! I'M IGOR, THE INVISIBLE MAIL CARRIER!
UMM... I SEE! WELL, MAKE YOURSELF COMFORTABLE!

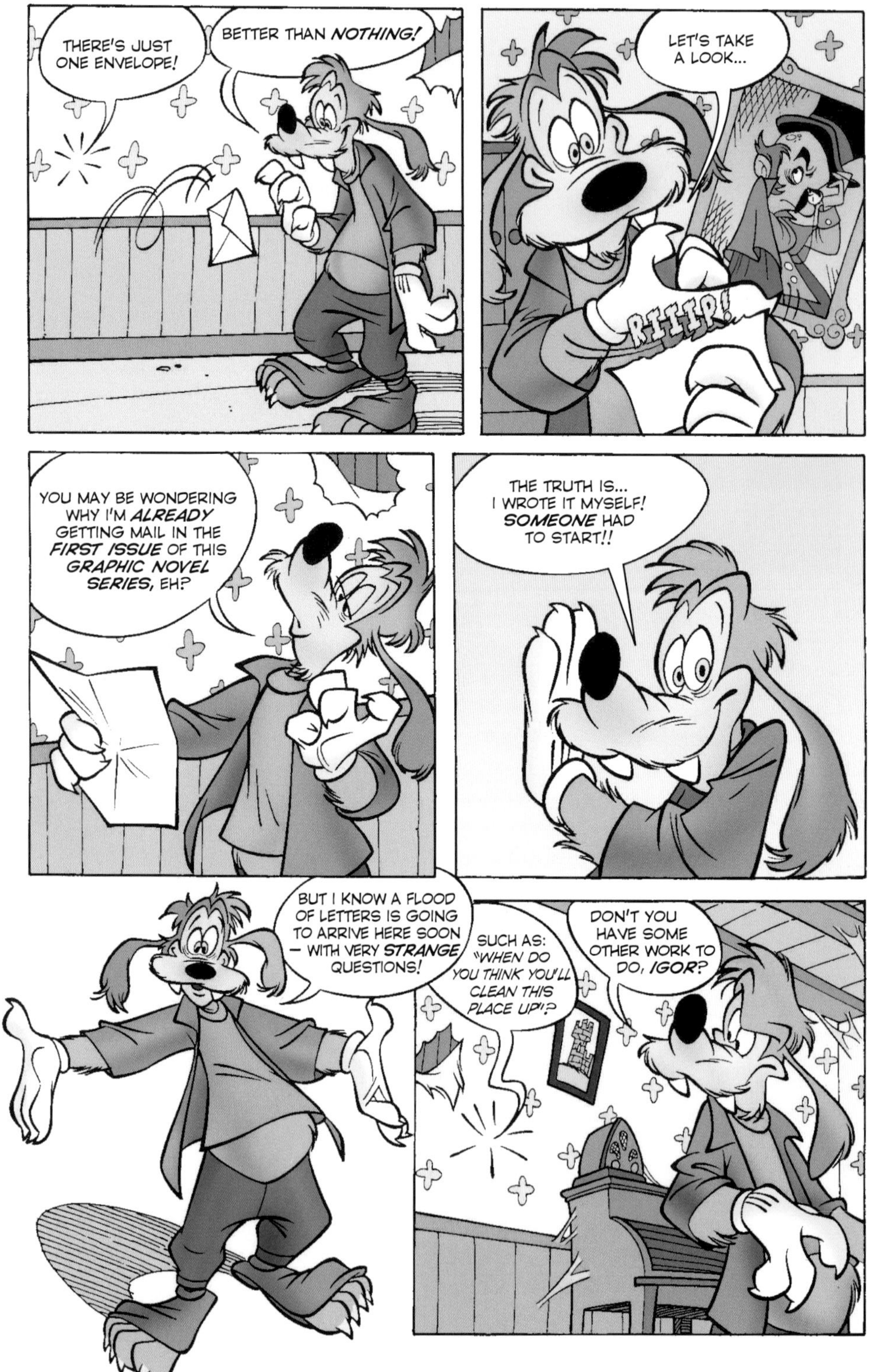

THERE'S JUST ONE ENVELOPE!
BETTER THAN *NOTHING!*
LET'S TAKE A LOOK...
RIIIP!
YOU MAY BE WONDERING WHY I'M *ALREADY* GETTING MAIL IN THE *FIRST ISSUE* OF THIS *GRAPHIC NOVEL SERIES,* EH?
THE TRUTH IS... I WROTE IT MYSELF! *SOMEONE* HAD TO START!!
BUT I KNOW A FLOOD OF LETTERS IS GOING TO ARRIVE HERE SOON — WITH VERY *STRANGE* QUESTIONS!
SUCH AS: *"WHEN DO YOU THINK YOU'LL CLEAN THIS PLACE UP"?*
DON'T YOU HAVE SOME OTHER WORK TO DO, *IGOR?*

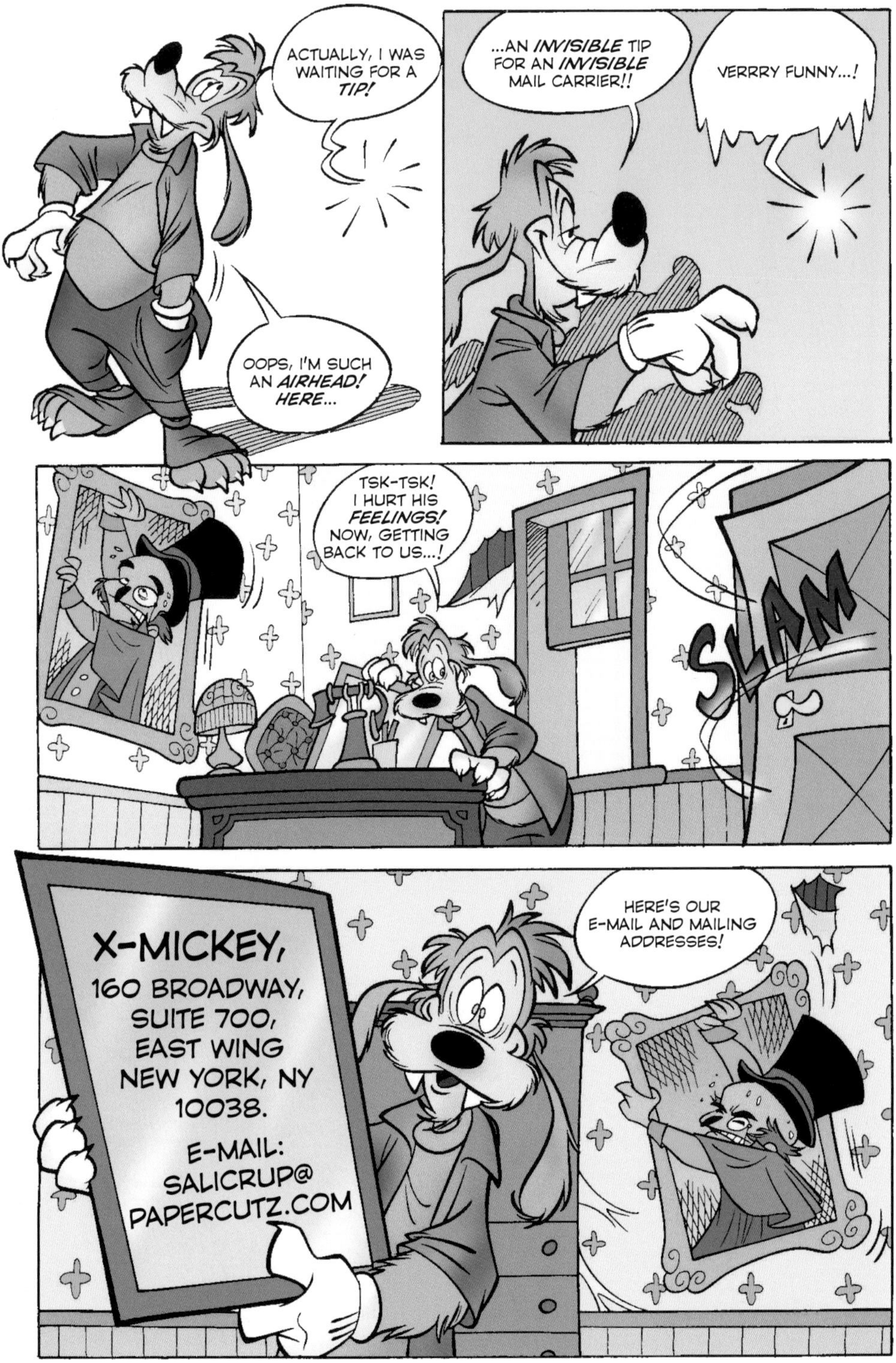
ACTUALLY, I WAS WAITING FOR A TIP!
OOPS, I'M SUCH AN AIRHEAD! HERE...
...AN INVISIBLE TIP FOR AN INVISIBLE MAIL CARRIER!!
VERRRY FUNNY...!
TSK-TSK! I HURT HIS FEELINGS! NOW, GETTING BACK TO US...!
SLAM
HERE'S OUR E-MAIL AND MAILING ADDRESSES!
X-MICKEY,
160 BROADWAY,
SUITE 700,
EAST WING
NEW YORK, NY
10038.
E-MAIL:
SALICRUP@
PAPERCUTZ.COM

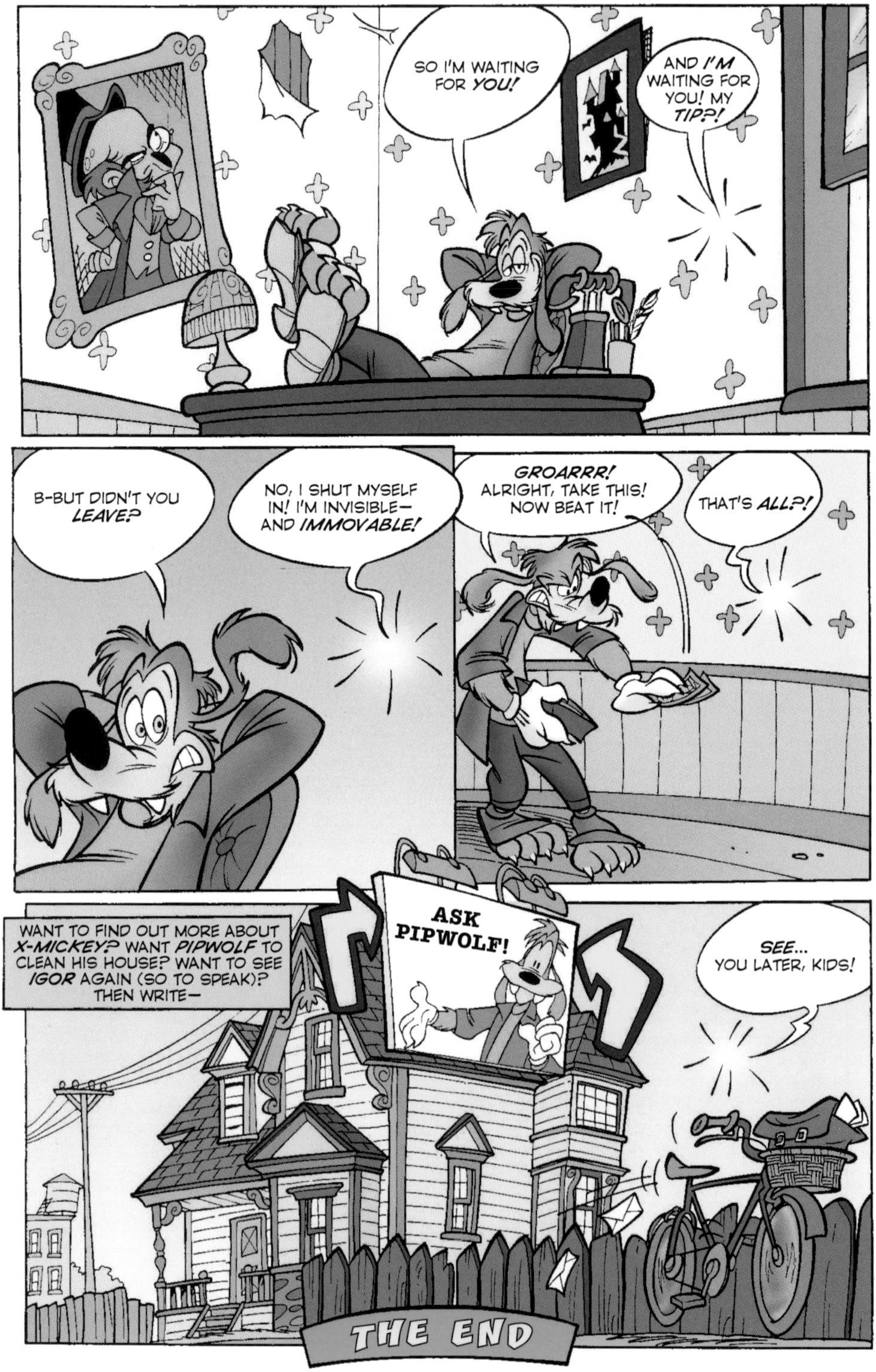
SO I'M WAITING FOR YOU!
AND I'M WAITING FOR YOU! MY TIP?!
B-BUT DIDN'T YOU LEAVE?
NO, I SHUT MYSELF IN! I'M INVISIBLE— AND IMMOVABLE!
GROARRR! ALRIGHT, TAKE THIS! NOW BEAT IT!
THAT'S ALL?!
WANT TO FIND OUT MORE ABOUT X-MICKEY? WANT PIPWOLF TO CLEAN HIS HOUSE? WANT TO SEE IGOR AGAIN (SO TO SPEAK)? THEN WRITE—
ASK PIPWOLF!
SEE... YOU LATER, KIDS!
THE END